rain and revelation

For Catherine,
A new friend ~
I hope you enjoy
all the best,

rain and revelation

Therese Pautz

This book is a work of fiction. Names, characters, places, and incidents either are products of the author's imagination or are used fictitiously. Any resemblance to actual events or locales or persons, living or dead, is entirely coincidental.

ISBN: 978-0615718798

Printed in the United States of America
Book design by Ryan Scheife, Mayfly Design
Typeset in Whitman
First Printing: 2012

16   15   14   13   12 5   4   3   2   1

Published by Beyond Eden Press, LLC

To my mother, Elizabeth Jane Pautz

Prologue

The rain and howling wind drown out the sounds of life in Louisburgh, a small west-coast village forgotten on sightseeing tours of Ireland. No one occupies the village square at the corner of Long Street and Bridge Street. No lights are shining in the windows of the terraced, two-story buildings abutting each other and perched near the curb; only the faint glow from the streetlights. Curtains remain drawn. Only a few cars and emptied, steel kegs nestle the curbs. Even the dogs, normally roaming and looking for a friendly rub or a handout, take cover inside.

Not far from the square, tucked down a quiet road on the rocky, landscaped knoll, sits a cluster of holiday cottages. All are vacant except one, from which a light is barely visible through the four-paned window. Rainwater cascades across the slate roof that replaced the thatched one years ago and forms a muddy pool.

Inside, Annie Conroy worries about staining the white cast iron tub.

Earlier, she moved the bleach and a pile of neatly folded rags from the cabinet underneath the kitchen sink and put them in a plastic bucket. She folded yellow rubber gloves over the bucket's lip. Then she put the bucket near the pedestal sink. It would be easier to clean up the mess. For years, she tried to bleach the tub, but it still looked like the discolored tap water. It should have been replaced years ago. But, she never asked for anything.

Except this morning, Annie asked her husband, Seamus, to sharpen the boning knife before he left to tend the sheep and then to drive to Dublin with his mate, Paddy.

Annie knows a clean cut makes all the difference.

Lying in the empty tub, Annie looks out the window. Her daughter, Eliza, won't be home for hours. There's time. The rain's relentless drumming on the panes sounds a familiar lullaby. She closes her eyes and waits.

Death simply invited her home and she accepted.

Chapter One

I never told Ma I wouldn't be home last night or answered her calls. Now there's no time to stop home. I'm late in replacing the night attendant at my grandma and granda's B&B, which is off the main square in Louisburgh.

The raw wind and rain slams my face and stings my bloodshot eyes as I squint and strain to see a few feet ahead. At the door to the B&B, I can hardly see the keyhole through the water assaulting my face and dripping from my unwashed hair. The lock finally turns, and I dash inside. It's seven thirty. I'm a half hour late.

Maeve Cunningham, the night attendant, bristles past me. "Nice of you to make it, Eliza." She unfolds a clear plastic cap that she digs out of the zippered outside pocket of her handbag that looks a lot like my grandma's. She drapes it over her mousy, flat hair, and ties it under her second chin. As Maeve buttons the snug wool jacket, she says, "Oh, the guests need lunches. Bike tour at nine o'clock."

"Too busy to make them?"

"Something like that." Maeve juts her chin forward. Narrowing her beady eyes, she says, "Got kids to tend to. People who need me."

My head throbs from too many pints, and my stomach recoils at the whiff of Maeve's pungent body odor when she thrusts an envelope at me.

"This is for Mr. O'Donnell." Maeve never referred to him as my grandfather.

"He's on holiday, and I'm tending matters. What is it?" I can't help adding a tone of self importance that I know will stoke the fire of her discontent. Despite my protestations, Granda hired Maeve for the night duty because he felt sorry for her with the twin babies and her husband, Bobby, not working.

"My hours." Maeve waves the envelope at me.

I take it and toss it onto the counter. "I'll see that he gets it."

"You do that." Maeve's eyes, dark as coal, seem to disappear into her face as she glares at me. She reminds me of a bull, penned and ready to charge the ring. Her nostrils quiver. Then she turns, slings her bag over her shoulder, and slams the door behind her.

Maeve, six years older, talks to me only when she has to, especially since her brother, Mikey, took a fancy to me. That was two years ago, right before school ended and most of our classmates went to university. Mostly we're off, but sometimes we can't help ourselves. Always a mistake.

Taking off my raincoat, I go into the kitchen to prepare breakfast and the lunches.

Lace curtains hang over the vertical, deep-set windows. The sun, usually peeking out in the March sky by now, is hidden behind dark clouds.

My phone buzzes. Ma. Again. "When will you be home? Let me know." Only Ma texts in full sentences. Sighing, I toss my phone onto the counter without replying. How many other twenty-year-olds have mothers who have to know their whereabouts all the time?

Taking the homemade bread from the metal bread drawer, I line up slices on the wooden cutting board. Using the serrated knife, I begin cutting off the golden, hard crusts. The sight of food causes my stomach to lurch. The knife nicks the tip of my thumb. A chunk of raw flesh is exposed. Blood drips onto the white bread. Sucking the tip of my thumb to catch the blood, I reach into the cabinet near the sink for a bandage. I secure it tightly. Blood discolors the bandage. I apply another one on top of it. My thumb throbs. The clock's ticking echoes. Finally, grabbing a pair of disposable gloves from the box on the counter, I begin again, carefully holding my thumb up, trying to relieve the pulsating pain.

Heavy footsteps clomp down the wooden stairs as I finish making the lunches. The guests amble into the living room, and I hurry out to greet them.

They ask when the rain will end. Never, I want to say. Instead, I assure them it could stop anytime. Spring on the west coast of Ireland is like that. Things change. Sometimes without warning. Best to stay flexible and prepare for all conditions, I tell them with a wink and a smile.

The guests stare out the window and don't seem to notice when I leave to get the place settings and food. A grey, colorless sky and sheets of rain shade from their view the rolling green hills, stone fences, and Clew Bay.

I notice that Ma sent another text, asking when I might be home. I reply, "When I am." Then I fling the phone back onto the counter. It slides off and lands on the floor. The battery pops off. When I bend down to get it, my stomach flips and my head whirls. I grip the counter's edge and wait for

3

the room to stop spinning and my stomach to recede from my throat before I stand.

As I grip the counter, I smell Mikey. On me. In me. Musty and stale.

Pulling my thick, damp hair into a ponytail, I notice my reflection in the small mirror hanging near the back door. Hair the color of chestnuts. Large green eyes. Pale skin. Dark circles. Cheekbones jutting out. I stare for a moment. At least I don't look as old as Maeve.

Relentless as the rain, the guests pepper me with questions while they eat breakfast. They can't decide where to go next. Masking my face with a smile, I listen to them prattle endlessly about their "rich discoveries and experiences among such charming, hospitable people" while traveling around Ireland. Finally, they decide to pack, take the lunches, and move on.

My phone rings just as I finish cleaning up and saying goodbye to the guests. I know immediately by the ringtone and time who it is. "Hallo, Granda."

"Everything go smoothly this morning?" Granda's voice booms through the phone. In the background are voices. Grandma's voice, like a squawking bird, dominates. They are on holiday in Italy, where they have another home near Naples.

I plop onto the couch facing the fake fire and close my burning eyes. "They've left. Shitty weather. Still."

How I wish I had a smoke to settle my stomach. But I gave my last pack to Mikey months ago. All done, I told him. I couldn't run with my lungs burning with each breath.

Still, I missed the way my lungs filled with each long drag and then let the smoke out slowly, sometimes in circles that floated to the void.

Granda sighs. "I was counting on the long reservation. Anything new come in?"

"Not since we talked yesterday."

"I've been trying to reach your father. He hasn't returned my calls. Does he ever carry his phone with him? He needs to make sure the cottages are ready for the Americans. They will be here soon, you know."

Granda says something else, but I can't make it out. He has turned his attention to Grandma, who is trying to tell him something. I close my eyes and wait. There is always more.

"I need you to do something. Go to my house and get some insurance documents for the cottages and fax them to me here. The key to the fire safe, which is under my bed, should be at your house on the key ring I gave to your mother before I left. It's the smaller key. Do this right off."

"Can't it wait until I get some sleep?"

"Night is for sleeping." Granda tells me to wait and muffles the phone. When he comes back, he says, "I need the fax within the hour. Bye, love."

I let the phone drop onto the cushion. For a few minutes I lay there, breathing deeply, trying to gauge whether the rain is letting up. My eyes feel heavy. I force my eyes open, sit up and hold my head in my hands. The room no longer spins, but I feel weighed down from too many pints and not enough sleep.

I debate only for a minute whether Granda can wait, but I know he can't. He prides himself as the only successful businessman among farmers. Everyone knows him. Everyone jumps when he asks for something. He's always polite and always smiles. He just does not wait.

~~~~~

Mikey picked me up last night so I have no car in town. I run into the biting wind and rain, barely able to see, but guided by feet that know the route by heart to the cottages that Granda owns just on the outskirts of town.

When I near home, drenched to the core, I don't see any lights on in our cottage. Da's pickup truck is gone. Only my car is there. Water spills over the empty planters under the window and onto the overgrown, weedy grass.

Entering the dark, dank cottage, I flip on the wall switch and the overhead light comes on in the kitchen above the wood-planked table. The whitewashed walls and fireplace are discolored by too many peat fires. The sink is empty, and the counters are bare, except for the teapot and cutlery block in the corner. The dish rag is neatly folded over the faucet.

There is no sign that anyone is home. There's only the familiar scent of bleach. Ma's been cleaning. Again.

Tossing my raincoat on the hook near the door, I flip off my knee-high wellies. They miss the mat, but I leave them where they land, scattered near the door. Cold from the stone floor rises through my feet and up my legs. Scurrying to the hearth rug, I don't see embers smoldering. There are no peat turves stacked next to the fireplace. My breath forms in front of me.

Hollering for Ma, I walk toward my bedroom, down the narrow hall off the living room. I flip on the light in my room. Pushing aside my hair, I look into the mirror above the dresser. Two round hickeys. I brush my fingers over them.

Still tender. I pull the sweater's cowl higher. It reeks of lager and cigar smoke. I debate bathing before going to Granda's. It might wake me up and get rid of the stench.

In the hallway leading to the bathroom, everything is dark. There is no light in my parents' room, but I can see in the shadows their neatly made bed.

There is no sign of Ma. She's not sitting at the kitchen table or lying on her bed, as she is when she's not cleaning. She's not cooking food that is filling but tasteless. She is not calling out to me, asking me where I've been and where I'm going.

There is a pale light coming from under the bathroom door at the end of the hall, but there is no sound of running water or movement. The only sound comes from the wind and rain battering the cottage.

"Ma?" No answer.

I knock on the door. It creaks open just a hair. I push the door open further. Grey light filters in through the glass block window, filling the bathroom that barely fits one person.

Then I see Ma slouched in the white cast iron tub. There's no water. Her straight, shoulder length hair is pulled back in two slides. The grey streaks near her temples stand out against her black hair. Her eyes stare at me. Wide. Vacant. Her mouth, open, is speechless.

Blood is pooling in Ma's sunken abdomen. Some trickles down Ma's narrow hips. Her naked body, stretched but not filling the empty tub, blends into the porcelain except for her black, grey-streaked hair falling onto her shoulders.

Chapter Two

I stand in the doorway looking in. Frozen.

Ma's eyes, wide and deep set, stare past me at the light. Her thin, parted lips twitch. It looks like she's going to say something. But no words come out. Her eyes close. I can see her ribs as her chest rises, then lowers. Across her small, saggy breasts lies a shiny knife. She has her right hand on the black handle, almost clutching it.

Ma's hand moves. A jerk. More blood. The knife clangs against the side of the tub. Jarred, I lurch forward and yell, "Oh, my God! No!" One step takes me to the edge of the cast iron tub. My knee hits the claw foot. Grabbing the hand towel near the basin, I slap it on Ma's wrist. Blood leaks through. I grab the thicker towel on the rack and wrap it tightly.

With my hand clamping down on the towel, I whip my head around, looking for something. What? Someone to come. Someone to help. Someone to tell me that this is not real; that it is a hallucination, a dream. But, there is no one else.

And there is no time.

With one hand on the blood-soaked towel, I dig with my other hand for my phone in my back pocket. I stare at it. Who can I call? There is no doctor or clinic in town and no ambulance to call that could get here in time. The closest hospital is in Castlebar, a forty-five minute drive in good weather.

Rushing into my parents' room, I grab the white chenille bedspread and drag it into the bathroom. I lift her out of the tub, straining to keep the towel on her wrist, and collapse on the tiled, ceramic floor with her in my arms. Wrapping her in the blanket, I clutch her close to me. A soft groan rises from her parted mouth. Rocking back and forth, I tell her to hold on. Her breath is warm on my cheek. She feels limp and small, almost like a child, not a grown woman. Not my mother.

My mother would never do this.

As my heart pounds, my breath quickens. Tears flood my face. No words of comfort or pleas come out of my mouth. Mute, I try to think of what to do.

There is only one thing I can do. Drive to Castlebar and pray that there's still time.

Chapter Three

Ma feels like a sack of potatoes slung over my shoulder, wrapped in the bedspread that I've pulled tight around her. I'm afraid I'll drop her. It's her faint breath in the nape of my neck that weighs me down. Still warm. I wait for each breath. Still there. I hold my breath until I feel the next one.

Rain pummels us as I carry her to my car, the rusting Ford Escort parked near the door. I try to protect her from the rain, but her naked body in the bedspread is penetrable, defenseless.

I lower Ma into the backseat. Limp, like a sleeping newborn, her body doesn't move. It stays where I lay her. She doesn't curl up. I bend her legs so she will fit, and scatter the magazines and running clothes so they aren't by her face. Pale and barely visible in the blanket, her face doesn't look peaceful or in pain. It doesn't, I realize, look like the mother I thought I knew.

The wipers struggle to scatter the rain pounding the cracked windshield. Sitting hunched over, my hands clenching the wheel, I can barely see a few feet ahead of me on the road to Castlebar.

My chest constricts. It feels like my breath is being squeezed out. I look for sheep. For cars. For time to be on our side. The pounding rain and furious wipers beat in my head. I look in the rearview mirror. Ma lays motionless. I don't know if she's still breathing. The spot on my neck where I felt her breath is cold. I crank the heat. I never noticed how the car takes bumps, its shocks useless. It seems like I've been driving for hours. I glance at the clock. Ten o'clock. I have been driving twenty minutes.

A light on the side of the road catches my eye. It spotlights a wooden, engraved sign with white painted lettering: Westport Veterinary Clinic. Pumping my brakes, I slow, barely making the turn into the gravel lot. The car skids to a stop. Ma bumps the front seat. In the mirror I see her mouth open slightly, but no words come out. Her eyes are still shut.

Quickly I get out, open the rear door and lower my face to her mouth. At first I don't feel anything. My gut clenches. Then I feel her faint breath. It's softer, it seems, than before. Lower, near her side, where I've wrapped her wrist in towels, I see that blood is soaking through the white bedspread.

I run into the clinic through the sheets of rain and scattered puddles. Barging through the door into the reception area, I yell for Doc, who helps Da during lambing. My voice doesn't sound like my own. It's higher, louder and frantic. A man, who is talking to the receptionist, moves out of my way.

Leaning on the counter, I repeat to the woman behind the desk, "I need Doc. Quick. My ma's in the car." I turn, not looking to make sure she heard me or to see if anyone is coming.

When I get to the car, the man who was standing at the counter talking to the receptionist is behind me. Wearing only a wool shirt and jeans but no overcoat, he lowers his lanky body into the rear seat. "Holy Mother Mary, what happened?" He is touching Ma's neck with his hand.

The rain pours over me. "She cut her wrist."

Without a word he lifts Ma out of the car and carries her toward the clinic. He yells, "Get the door!"

Inside he barks, "Call an ambulance. Get Imogene." I follow him to the door, but the receptionist rises and plants her body between him and me. With her hair standing as tall as her hips spread wide, she blocks me from following. I look past her girth, but the door closes and Ma and the man disappear.

"Let him take her. You come with me, dear." She grips my arm and steers me down a hall to a windowless room numbered two. A pedestal exam table fills the room. Mounted above the polished, stainless steel top is a computer monitor with a screensaver of sleeping golden retriever puppies curled together. There are wood cabinets mounted above the sink. On the counter beneath the cabinets is a bottle of disinfectant and clear, glass canisters with dog bones and cotton gauzes. I sit down on one of the metal chairs in my soaked jeans and sweater. I never grabbed my jacket. It dawns on me that I never shut the cottage door. Shuddering, I stare at the dull linoleum floor scattered with my muddied prints. I can't stop shaking.

The woman drapes a blanket over my shoulders. "Can I get you anything, dear?" I can smell her breath ripe from cigarettes and coffee. I shake my head and look at the door, straining to see or hear anything that would tell me what was happening. She lowers herself into the other chair. Her polyester-covered thighs spill over the unpadded chair. Touching my arm, she whispers, "Dr. McCullough will take care of her."

"That's not Doc McCullough." I jerk my head back toward the closed door.

"'Tis his son, Ryan. He just joined us. Right out of school."
Her voice swells with pride.

I try to picture the man's face, but can't. Young. That's all
I recall.

Doors slam shut somewhere down the hall. There are
voices and words that I can't make out. They rise and fall. I
try imagining what is going on with Ma, but can't. I strain to
hear the sound of sirens. There are none.

"Would you like me to pray with you, dear?" She reaches
for my hands which are stained with Ma's blood. I yank them
back, fold them in my lap and shake my head. "I'm really
fine. Thank you."

She smiles in a sugary way. "Then I'll get you something
hot to drink. Just wait here, love." With her trousers riding
high, the woman waddles away. The hollow door shudders
shut.

Why would Ma do something like this? Squeezing my
eyes shut, I see stars. Then a red glow. Quickly I open my eyes.

I think back to yesterday. Everything seemed fine when
I came home after my afternoon run. She was sitting at the
table. Her spot. I don't recall our conversation, except she
asked if I would be home for dinner. I said, "I don't think
so." I couldn't tell her that Mikey was picking me up, and we
were meeting Fiona at Paddy's pub after Maeve replaced me
at the B&B. Ma liked Fiona, but not Mikey. She never liked
any of my boyfriends. She just nodded without looking at me.
She didn't try to make me feel guilty for not eating. Mostly
she wanted to know when I'd be home.

She always wanted me home, and I always wanted to be
somewhere else.

A siren silences my thoughts. Feet pound past the closed door, down the hall. Should I leave or stay put? I stand frozen, staring at the shut door. Voices, muted but urgent, disappear. There's a buzz of activity, but I am forgotten.

Then the door swings open, nearly hitting me before I step back. The man who carried Ma from the car stands there with his brow furrowed and his freckled face framed in brown curls.

"They're loading her now." He steps aside, motions me out toward the lobby area and then puts his hand on the low of my back and steers me out the front door.

"Is she still...?"

He nods.

Two attendants are about to close the ambulance's rear door. Its blue lights are flashing. I can see Ma strapped to the gurney. She's covered in layers of blankets. An oxygen mask covers her face.

"Hold on," Doc's son tells them.

They turn. He tilts his head toward me. They take my hands and hoist me inside and I mutter thanks.

I fall into a seat in the rear, away from the attendants who hook Ma to a monitor. I watch lines on the monitor without comprehending their meaning. The red lights flicker. Ma's chest rises and then collapses. The attendant grabs something—I'm not sure what—from the white metal cabinets.

The door slams shut. I grip the seat. My knuckles turn white as the ambulance jolts forward.

Chapter Four

The last thing I remember is the doors of the ambulance slamming shut with Ma and me inside, and the piercing siren. Now the doors are open and I'm still slumped in the jumpseat. An attendant is hovering over me.

I don't see Ma.

"What happened?" My voice sounds like a croaky whisper as I straighten up.

The attendant tapes the gauze down on the side of my head. "You fainted just after we took off and hit your head on the metal corner of the cabinet."

Touching my head, I cringe and prop myself up. "I need to find Ma."

He puts his supplies aside, jumps out of the ambulance, and extends his hand. I feel wobbly for a minute, but he steadies me. He asks if I'm okay walking through the emergency room door on my own, or do I need a wheelchair? I thank him, tell him I'm fine and walk the few feet to the door.

The rain has stopped, but dark clouds hover. A gust of wind whips my hair into my eyes. A strand catches in the tape and I nearly pull the bandage off when I tug the hair free.

Inside, fluorescent lights hurt my eyes. I can't see Ma, only people standing in the hall, huddled in conversation.

Then I see a desk. Behind it sits a grey-haired woman with a tight perm. She's explaining something to an elderly couple. I stand behind them. The man, clutching his walker, jokes about the football team's botched game. They don't seem to notice me. His wife digs through papers with no sense of urgency.

Finally it's my turn. "My ma just came in. I need to find her. Annie Conroy's her name."

The woman smiles and slides a clipboard with papers towards me. "Please take these papers, fill them out and then bring them back." She spots someone wheeling a cart and waves. A chuckle escapes from her mouth as she looks down and begins typing something on the computer.

My breath quickens. "Do you know if she's okay?"

She looks up. "I'm not sure, Miss, but we will find out. First, fill out the forms."

"She just came in with the ambulance." I consider lowering my voice, but don't. "*Please*, can you tell me where they took her?"

"I don't know, but don't worry. She's in good hands and someone will attend to you shortly." She looks to the people behind me and waves them forward.

I don't move. "Can *you* check?" The couple that was ahead of me stops a few feet away. They whisper to each other like people do when you come late to Mass and have to sit in the front pew.

She pushes the clipboard closer. In a deep, measured tone she says, "If you could *please* fill out the papers, Miss, I can help you. And, these fine people, too." She motions towards chairs lining the wall.

I grab the clipboard and nearly knock over a cart of flowers. I mumble an apology and sit in the only open chair. Sandwiched between a woman cradling a crying infant with snot running down her red, blotchy face, and a long-haired boy dressed all in black, staring out the window with a set jaw, I start filling out the form.

Name of Patient: Annie Marie Conroy.

Reason for visit: Cut.

Date. I stop. What day is it? I fumble in my bag, digging for my phone, to check the date. I write the date, then stop and stare at what I've just written. It can't be.

It's Ma's birthday. Her fortieth.

The fact that her birthday was approaching never crossed my mind. She hated her birthday or any fussing over her. Why would she do this today? Why would she do this at all?

I finish the forms and return the clipboard and forms, and then return to my seat as directed, to wait for news.

I call Da. He doesn't answer. No surprise. I consider calling Paddy's phone since he usually picks up, but instead I leave a message for Da saying that Ma cut herself and is at the hospital in Castlebar. I tell him to call me right away and to get here quick. I hang up but then call back and tell him that I don't know if Ma will make it. I try not to sound like I'm crying. I try sounding like I'm okay. I make it short because my battery is almost dead.

I wait without any word about Ma. The woman with the baby and the boy leave and others claim their seats. The person distributing chipboards finally reports that they are attending to Ma, but she knows nothing else.

Granda calls. Four times. Each time I let it go into voice-mail. I know what he wants, but I can't bear to call him back when I don't have any news.

17

I sit and stare at the door where I think they took Ma. I've seen other people come in on stretchers and get wheeled through the windowless, grey door.

Hours pass.

Finally a speckled, older man calls my name. I raise my hand like I'm back in school and then walk toward him. He looks gravely at me over his glasses and says, "I'm Dr. O'Brien and I've been attending to your mother."

"Is she..."

"Weak, but stabilized."

"Will she live?"

"She lost a lot of blood, but she should." He looks past me to the people occupying the row of chairs. "Is your father here?"

"Not yet. Soon. I think."

He nods. "I'll be back when I have more news." Then he disappears behind the unmarked doors.

I stand there alone.

Then I spot Styrofoam cups and a steel container of coffee and go pour myself a cup. It is thick, black and bitter. I can't drink it. Sitting back in the chairs, I wait. On the far wall is a mounted television. I don't recognize the show. Others in the room stare at it, too. Luckily, no one tries to talk to me. My eyes feel heavy, and my head throbs.

I must have dozed off because a familiar voice booms and jars me awake.

"Where the hell is my wife?"

Staggering through the sliding glass doors is my disheveled father, followed by Paddy, his best mate. I intercept Da. He steadies himself on the wall and looks at me blurry-eyed. "My Eliza," he slurs.

"Nice of you to finally get here." My face is close enough

that his grey stubble scratches my cheek. His breath reeks of cigars and whiskey.

"How is she?" Paddy leans in to kiss me.

Da staggers to the chairs. A family promptly vacates. "You sounded so serious." He contorts his face and tries focusing his bloodshot eyes on my face.

"It is serious," I say, my teeth clenched.

Paddy stares intently at me. "What happened?"

"She slit her wrist in the tub." My voice cracks.

Da wails, "Oh, bloody hell."

"It was." My tone is sharp.

Paddy puts his arm around me, and I cry. I don't want to, but I can't stop. I bury my head in his wool overcoat that smells sweet and familiar. He strokes my hair. After a few minutes he points to the bandage on my forehead. "What happened to you?"

"It's nothing, just a bump. I fainted in the ambulance." I pull away when I hear footsteps.

Dr. O'Brien says to Paddy, "Mr. Conroy?"

Da nearly tips over as he gets up. "I'm Seamus Conroy. Not that bloke."

As Dr. O'Brien shakes Da's hand, Paddy puts his hands in his suit pockets and steps a few feet back and looks down at his polished shoes.

"Your wife lost a lot of blood, but luckily your daughter got her to a clinic in time to stop the bleeding. She is stabilized, but we are still watching her closely."

"Aye, Eliza's a smart one." He takes off his tweed hat and runs his hands through his flattened brown hair.

Paddy clears his throat and steps forward. "I'm a friend of the family. Paddy McDonald." He shakes Dr. O'Brien's hand.

Dr. O'Brien steers us down the hallway, outside the hearing of others waiting for news. "I've recommended that Mrs. Conroy be admitted to St. Patrick's Hospital in Dublin. They do an excellent job treating people with depression and have an in-patient program for which she qualifies. I've already been in contact with them, and they can admit her once we are confident she can travel."

"Annie's always been a bit off in the head, but she's not a nut job," Da bellows. Paddy grabs his arm and tells him to mind himself.

Dr. O'Brien grimaces. He says, "Mr. Conroy, your wife needs help. This isn't the first time she has done this."

"What?" I say.

Dr. O'Brien turns to me. "There are scars on her other wrist. It doesn't look like it was a deep cut, but still I am concerned that if she doesn't receive treatment, she may try to harm herself again."

Da shakes his head. "Hell, that was when she was a wee thing. She was just twelve or thirteen. Just playing around, she said." Da turns to Paddy. "Didn't she tell us about that? Her ma was pissed and gave her a beating for it. Remember?" Paddy shrugs.

"I don't think she's playing around, Mr. Conroy. She needs help."

"Jaysus. What will people say? They talk, you know."

I swat the sleeve of Da's jacket, which nearly knocks him over. Paddy steps forward and steadies Da.

I say, "Can I see her?"

Dr. O'Brien shakes his head. "I'm afraid she doesn't want to see anyone, including you and your father. I'm sorry. She has agreed to go to St. Patrick's—so, Mr. Conroy, your permission is not necessary."

Da huffs and staggers back to the chairs. With cap askew, he stretches and closes his eyes.

Dr. O'Brien digs out a piece of paper from his pocket and holds it out to me. "It's an excellent facility. Here is the name of the contact person. They will arrange transfer."

I take the paper. The small, nearly illegible writing blurs through a veil of tears. I nod. Paddy thanks the doctor, who excuses himself to see other patients.

Tucking the paper in my pocket, I turn toward the door. "I'm out of here."

Paddy puts his arm out and stops me. "How are you getting back? Let me drive all of us home." He tries to hug me, but I dodge his embrace and shake off his sympathy. Casting a glance at Da, I see he's now spread himself over two chairs and has closed his eyes.

"Don't mind me. I'll take care of myself."

I walk outside, through the now empty hall and out the main entrance. Then, I call Mikey.

Chapter Five

The mist cools my puffy, tired eyes as I sit on the bench across the street from the hospital. In the shadows, under the burned-out street lamp, I wait for Mikey. It's nearly eight o'clock now. Eventually Da and Paddy come out. They don't see me. Paddy is holding Da up and saying something that I can't make out because the wind has picked up and is whistling through the trees. They get into Paddy's car.

I watch Paddy's taillights disappear.

Mikey O'Neal eventually shows up, sounding his horn and pulling over. He lowers the window and smiles. "Fancy a lift?"

I walk around and open the door of the car. It creaks. A carton of Benson and Hedges, mud-caked work gloves, and an assortment of candy and crisp wrappers clutter the stained cloth seat. Pushing them aside, I get in. On the floor is a six-pack of Harp.

Mikey leans over and kisses me, but I don't kiss him back.

He pouts. "Why the puss face, love?"

"How do you expect me to look after everything?"

He stares at me blankly.

"Did you even listen to my message?" I snap the seat belt into place, cross my arms and glare at him.

"Ah, it was so long." He reaches for my hand and puts it in on his crotch. "But a little Mikey love can fix anything. You know that."

When I yank my hand away and move closer to the door, he grins and leans over. Entwining his fingers in my long hair, he kisses my neck and whispers, "I missed you."

I push him away, and he looks at me like I slapped him. I pull my sweater up to cover the hickeys from last night.

"That's a fine thanks for driving all the way over here to get you."

Mikey stares ahead, his face twisted in a scowl. He won't look at me. I know he's waiting for me to apologize. Sinking into the seat, I close my eyes. In a voice that sounds small and unlike my own, I say, "Ma tried to kill herself today. I just want to go home, okay?"

"Oh, God!" He tries to touch me, but I move closer to the door and look into the dark sky. When I tell him my car is at Doc McCullough's, he looks at me like I've just told him a dog had kittens. I simply rest my head on the seat and stare ahead.

Mikey puts the car in drive and takes off. My shoulder slams the passenger door when he whips the car around toward Louisburgh. An empty beer bottle rolls out from under the seat and hits my foot. I kick it aside, and we drive in silence.

When we get to the vet clinic, my car is the only one in the lot, and everything is dark except for the lit sign that caught my attention earlier.

Mikey kisses my cheek. "See you tonight?"

I shake my head. I say nothing even though there's much to say. I notice lines around his eyes. I can't remember when

I looked closely at my own face. Maybe I have lines, too, at twenty.

The car's headlights reveal scattered puddles, which I step over to get to my car. I hear the tires squeal as Mikey accelerates toward Louisburgh. Inside the car, I check my phone to see if Fiona has called or texted me, but she hasn't.

Driving home, I look for sheep but see only Ma's face as she lay in the tub and then covered with the oxygen mask in the ambulance. I force myself to stare ahead at the dark road. I can't recall a time I returned home and Ma wasn't sitting at the kitchen table or in the rocker with a cup of tea. I wonder what she's doing now, who's with her, and why she refused to see me.

When I get home, the front door is still open. I flip the wall switch and see the floor covered in rainwater. Slamming the door, I go and turn on every light in the living room and kitchen. Snatching towels from the hall closet, I toss them on the floor to soak up the water. The heavy drapes covering the windows remain closed.

My eyes fall on the painting of the Virgin Mary hanging on the wall in the living room. I never noticed how sad her eyes looked holding the baby Jesus. Cold seeps into my body.

I turn up the electric heat, but don't bother going outside to get more peat turves from the stack in back of the cottage. Instead, I walk around the overstuffed couch and the hand-carved rocker, into the kitchen and around the wood-planked table with the four straight-backed chairs, and back again.

As I walk around the cottage, I glance at the framed pictures on the fireplace mantel, on the end tables, and on the bookshelves on the far wall. They are all of me: an infant in my long christening gown with bright red hair sticking straight up; seven years old in my first communion dress with hair curly from being set in pink foam rollers; twelve years old in the knit jumper outfit Ma made for me with straight hair the color of chestnuts; and many more of me and Fiona, my best friend, as fairies, as princesses, and in our various dresses for the formal school dances. Da and Ma aren't in the pictures with me. There are no pictures of them together.

I walk the room as through a labyrinth. Everything looks the same, but different.

Something small on the window ledge, above the stainless steel kitchen sink, catches my attention. It's Ma's wedding ring: a Claddagh ring, two hands holding a crowned heart.

I slip the ring on my pinkie and stare at it. Ma never took her wedding ring off.

My phone buzzes, cutting the silence.

Fiona texts that she wants to meet up at the pub. I presume she listened to the message that I left her while I was waiting at the hospital, but she doesn't ask how Ma is or if she should come over. Not tonight, I reply. She texts that everyone is going out and asks me to change my mind. Maybe she didn't listen and doesn't know. I don't have the energy to call her and can't explain everything in text messages.

I walk down the hall toward the bathroom. Standing in the bathroom doorway, I see the blood streaks in the tub and on the floor where I held Ma. My eyes fall upon a bucket tucked under the pedestal sink. Yellow rubber gloves are folded over the bucket's lip. A bottle of bleach and an assortment of cloths cut from my old flannel pajamas fill the bucket.

Ma hates messes.

Putting on the gloves, I begin cleaning while tears stream down my face.

Chapter Six

My phone rings, jarring me awake. The sun peeks into my bedroom through the half-closed curtains. I'm on top of my still-made bed, dressed in the clothes I wore yesterday. Reaching for my phone on the nightstand, I answer it in a low, gravelly voice without looking to see who is calling.

"It's about time you answer your damn phone. I've been waiting for those documents," Granda's voice booms.

"Sorry." I sit up and hold my head in my hands. My thick hair falls into my face. It smells dirty.

"Do you think that you can bother yourself enough to do that now or should I have Maeve attend to it?" His tone is sharp.

"No, I'm back now and can do it."

"Back?"

"Ma." I fall into the mound of pillows. "She's in the hospital."

"What?"

I gulp, my mouth dry. "She tried to kill herself."

"Good lord." In a lowered voice, he says, "Is she..."

"Alive."

"Thank God."

"They're transferring her to Dublin. To a psychiatric hospital. They say she needs help so she won't do this again."

"Wait until I tell her mother. St. Patrick himself would throw a fit. Are you okay?"

I hug my legs. "Yeah."

"That's good." His voice softens. "I don't suppose it would help if I came home." There are clanging and rustling noises in the background, but no voices.

"I dunno."

"Well, keep me posted." It sounds like he's rummaging for something. "Now, when you can, could you please be a love and go to my house and fax those documents to me? Your mother had the keys on a ring. The small one is to the fire safe under the bed."

Before I can even answer he says, "Oh, and have your father call me. I need to know where we stand in getting the cottages ready for the Americans. I left him several messages."

"Right."

"Thanks, love. Ring me later when you know more about your mother."

I hang up and burrow beneath the down comforter. In the other room I hear the teapot whistling and Da's heavy boots clomping across the floor. I debate getting up to talk to him but don't. What is there to say? The front door finally slams shut.

After a few more minutes of lying there, I swing my legs over the bed and look out the window at a cloudless day. The brightness hurts my eyes. I strip off my clothes and slip into running gear neatly stacked on the chair with other freshly laundered clothes. After pulling my hair back into a pony-tail and tucking it under a cap, I sneak a look at the mirror. My face looks splotchy and my eyes are slits sandwiched between swollen lids and puffy bags. There is still a bump on my head from when I fainted.

The smell of buttered toast lingers in the kitchen, and a sweet peat fire warms the room. On the kitchen table is a plate with two scones still in the bag from the grocer. Da knows these are my favorites. I walk over and break off pieces of the scone, which melt in my mouth and satisfy my rumbling stomach.

Da's tackle box—the big one with the stacked containers—is open on the coffee table facing the smoldering fire. A spot on the oversized couch is sunken. There are piles of trout flies sorted according to size.

I walk over and pick one up. As a child, I used to love holding the flies, with their shiny bodies and feathery tails. Da taught me their names. On the table are some of my favorites: twinkle cat's whisker, orange zonker, wooly bugger, pink tadpole and woven olive damsel. I look out at Clew Bay, resting under a blanket of sun. The seemingly harmless fly that I'm holding by its plume shimmers in the light streaming through the windows.

After finding Granda's keys on a hook in the kitchen and zipping the small pocket in my jacket to secure them, I leave the cottage. I can see my breath as I begin my run. The ground, heavy with water from weeks of rain, cushions my steps as I run from our cottage down toward Clew Bay. A breeze blows, carrying the sounds of seagulls and waves lapping the rocky shore.

I put in my headphones and crank the music. The rusted bicycle propped against a sign to the beaches marks my turn to the narrow, beaten path that I run every day. It snakes through the rolling hills overlooking Clew Bay and then dips back down toward the Bunowen River. Sheep look over the rock fences and then turn away.

My legs feel tight, and my lungs burn from the cigarettes I bummed the other night from Mikey.

The winding path narrows. I nearly trip over an imbedded rock as I crane my head to see if Da is at his favorite fishing spot on the river. He is. I catch myself and regain my footing. From a distance, with his back to me, I watch the arc of his arm as he casts, dropping the line softly, trying to entice the brown trout. I quicken my pace.

Eventually I settle into a rhythm. My mind clears and I can breathe. I'm free. Except from the questions. Why did Ma try to kill herself when she was young? Why did she choose to do it again on her fortieth birthday? Why didn't I notice something was wrong with her? She acted the same as any day. What was different? Why would she take off her wedding ring? If she wanted to die, why do it that way? She hates messes. Why would she do this to me? She always said that she lives for me.

I run faster until I can't breathe.

When I arrive at my grandparents' house, my legs feel like jelly. Outside Louisburgh, in the new subdivision, their two-story house sits on an isolated cul-de-sac with a meticulously manicured lawn. I punch the code on the front door to get in and flip my shoes off on the rug. My socks slip on the highly-polished wood floor as I walk to the kitchen. I take off my jacket, fling it onto the marble countertop, and fill a glass with water from the dispenser. It cools my parched throat.

I don't dare sit down on the soft leather couch in my clothes soaked with perspiration.

Digging out the keys, I go to my grandparents' bedroom. I find the documents easily and slide the fire safe back under their bed, tuck the keys back into my pocket, and go to Granda's office down the hall.

As I fax the documents, I glance at the plaques on the wall and, on his desk, the framed picture of Granda receiving the County Mayo Good Citizen Award, taken just a few months ago. He stands in his dark suit, with broad shoulders and head held high, towering over the man shaking his hand. Nearly seventy, he looks half his age with his fit build and full head of thick red hair. "Hard work and clean living," he always told me—usually when I was doing neither.

The fax goes through. Job done. I'm free to leave.

A light mist is falling when I resume my run. When I'm nearly to town and finished with my playlist, I see Willie Walters pedaling his three-wheeled Schwinn down the street toward Sancta Maria College, the secondary school where he has taught music for as long as I can remember. He taught Ma and Da and he taught me. His dog, a stout black and white terrier named Johnny, is perched in the square wire basket behind the padded seat.

Mr. Walters lifts a finger in a wave. I take my headphones out of my ears. He stops. A cigar dangles from his mouth.

"Fine day for a run, Miss Conroy." Taking off his tweed cap, he runs his thick fingers through his sparse white hair. "Although I didn't expect to see you out. Not after everything."

I pet Johnny and avoid Mr. Walters's pale blue eyes, magnified behind his thick glasses. The dog jumps up on me, and I push him back down. I try to sound perky when I say, "It's nice to have sun finally."

Mr. Walters crosses his arms across his protruding belly, removes the cigar and points it at me. "I just heard from Paddy. 'Tis difficult, I'm sure."

30

Johnny wags his tail and nudges my hand when I stop petting him. "Everyone's fine, sir." I stroke the dog under his ears.

"Are *you*?" He peers over glasses perched on his bulbous nose.

Shrugging, I zip up my jacket to my chin. "I just don't know why she did it."

"We may never know. Even as a schoolgirl, your mother struggled." He smiles kindly. "You have her eyes you know."

A loud, rapid honking makes me jump.

Sean Murphy is waving from the driver's seat of the rickety yellow school bus taking up most of the road. He pulls up and opens the door. "You're just the person we're looking for." He turns back to the riders and bellows, "Meet Eliza Conroy." A few people wave while most stare ahead, glassy-eyed.

Sean mutters to me, "I got a message that their flight information transmitted wrong and they'd be arriving earlier than we planned. I left a message on your da's phone. Even tried your home and got no answer. So, here we are." When he smiles, he reveals his discolored, crooked teeth.

"You go," Mr. Walters says. "I'll stop by sometime and see how you are doing." He puts his cap back on and pedals toward the village square.

Climbing into the bus, I sit behind Sean on the duct-taped seat. Leaning in, I whisper, "Take them around. Do something. Go to Paddy's and tell him to give them free drinks. I need to make sure things are ready."

"Can't. My wee nephew's having his first communion this weekend, and I have to drive to Cork. My sister's throwing a bloody fit already that I'm late."

Sean talks a mile a minute as we bump down the uneven gravel road leading to the cottages. When we arrive at the turn, he cranks the wheel into the circular drive and then slams the brakes. I bump into his seat and hear groans from people in back.

The door to our cottage opens. Da walks out in his waders and fishing jacket. He smiles broadly. Walking to the bus, he says, "A fine welcome to you all."

The twenty American college students grip their backpacks and climb off the bus. Da winks and gives me the okay sign. He has things ready. I breathe more easily. As Da ushers them away to their new homes, I hear him tell them that he considers them family.

I'm barely inside our cottage long enough to take off my runners when my phone rings. It's Fiona. Her voice is high-pitched. "You must think I'm such an eejit for not coming. I got wasted last night and just listened to your message. Didn't even know you left one."

"You have other things than…"

"You kidding? Paddy just was in the store and told my ma. What can I do?"

"There's nothing to do."

I change the subject and tell her that the Americans arrived. She pummels me with questions that I don't know the answers to. No, I didn't get a good look at them. No, I don't know how many guys there are. No, there aren't more men than women. No, I don't know if they are going to the pubs tonight.

After much persuasion, Fiona convinces me to meet her at Paddy's pub later tonight. It is too hard to say no, and I really don't want to be alone. I need my best friend.

Chapter Seven

It's nearly ten o'clock when I get to Paddy's pub to meet up with Fiona. The wind catches the door behind me, slamming it shut. Inside the pub, it's warm and musty.

I expect to see the same people that I usually see on a Saturday night at Paddy's. Except, of course, the Americans might come out. Even with jet lag, usually there are a few who can't wait to experience the pubs and the locals.

Bobby Cunningham, Maeve's husband, is playing darts in the corner with his mates. He looks up at me when I come in, tilts his head in greeting and then tosses a dart that misses the board. He laughs and slugs his ale.

I look around. No Mikey. At least not yet.

I walk past Mr. Murphy, the chemist, who's sitting at a table with his wife. He sees me and says, "It was a nice day, hey?" I smile and agree. Mrs. Murphy arches her eyes and looks at me like she wants to say something, but she just looks down at the paper napkin she has folded into a small square. I tell them to enjoy their night out. Mr. Murphy says, "Couldn't get any better."

Fiona calls my name and waves from behind the mahogany bar. She's filling her glass with a shot of Jameson. Paddy, wiping down the glossy finish of the bar, looks up and smiles.

Tonight, he's making sure things look good for the Americans that are expected but not yet seen. Fiona squeezes past him.

"Darling, I'm so sorry about your ma." She hugs me with one arm, her glass held high in the other, and looks intently at me with her large fawn eyes that are heavily lined. "Let's sit. I need to know everything."

Fiona steers me past the old men playing canasta near the cast iron pot-bellied stove to a table near the front window overlooking Bridge Street. She asks in a low voice, "What the hell happened?"

"Just as I said." I lean back with my hands tucked in my jacket pockets. "There's nothing else to tell."

"But *why?*" Fiona takes a sip. Her lipstick imprints the whiskey glass.

"How would I know?" My tone is sharp. Fiona looks wounded. Softer, I say, "Sorry. There wasn't a note. Just her wedding ring on the kitchen windowsill. I have no idea what was going on in her head. I just found her. Now, she's in Dublin at a hospital and won't even see me."

"That sucks." Fiona takes a bigger swallow.

"She called that morning, and I didn't even answer." I look down. "I should have. Maybe I could have stopped her."

Fiona reaches over and touches my hand. "You're being too hard on yourself."

"Am I? Helluva daughter if you ask me." I reach over and take a gulp from her glass, which is nearly empty now. The whiskey warms my throat and soon the pub feels stuffy. I'm wearing jeans and a smart blouse that matches the silk scarf Ma gave me last year for my birthday. The scarf, wrapped around my neck, loosens and slips off when I take off my jacket.

"Nice hickeys." Fiona lets out a smug laugh. "Are you

gone in the head? He's a fine thing, but did you forget why you broke up with him?"

Shaking my head, I rewrap the scarf around my neck. "It was a mistake."

Fiona, the only one who knew the real reason I broke up with Mikey right after school ended, tilts her head toward the door. She says, "Well, don't look now. The mistake is here."

Mikey walks in, still wearing his work boots. He waves to Bobby. I get up and say to Fiona, "I need a jar. I'll be right back."

Fiona pushes her glass towards me. "Get me another." She digs in her bag, pulls out a compact mirror, and reapplies her lipstick. She hollers as I walk away, "Make it a double."

As I'm walking to the bar, Mikey comes over and puts his arm around my shoulder. His perspiration is mixed with cigarettes and an earthy smell from the potato farm he helps his father tend, receiving no wages. "Buying, love?" On the dole, he always looks to me—and to whomever is sitting on the next stool—for a drink.

I shake off his arm. In a voice that I think only he can hear, I say, "Buy your own. I'm not your 'love'; and we're forgetting what happened the other night, okay?"

He shoots me a wounded look. "Aw, but we were good together." He smiles in a way that long ago used to melt my heart.

In a low voice I say, "No, *I* was good for you. You weren't good for *me*. Didn't we find that out? Or, have you forgotten about when you weren't there for me." My eyes dare him to forget the child we almost had.

"Jaysus, do you got to bring that up all the time. That was ages ago. I would'a married you if I had to." He brushes my breast. "You have the best diddies." He laughs and takes a peak to see if his buddies caught it.

I push him away. "Thank the saints, we avoided that mistake. Now I'm avoiding another. Hump off." As I stride toward the bar, I hear him curse me, and the door slams shut. I breathe easier.

Paddy winks at me as I approach the men hunched on the bar stools with their hands gripping their drinks.

Paddy is standing behind the bar his grandfather carved. On the tobacco-stained walls are pictures of sports players and teams that Paddy, and his father before him, supported over the years. Several of the pictures are of Paddy and Da in their rugby uniforms.

"Hi sweetheart. The usual?" He flips the white towel over his shoulder.

"Yeah, but Fiona wants a double." I look back at Fiona. She's dressed in tight black trousers, high heeled leather boots and a fitted jacket that accentuates her ample chest and narrow waist. She's waiting, looking out the window.

Paddy reaches back for the bottle of Jameson from the shelf behind the bar. "I'm going to make her pay for them someday." He then pours me a pint of Harp and slides it to me. It tastes cool and goes down too smoothly.

Paddy refills it. "You okay?"

"Sure. Everything is grand." I force a smile.

"Finally got rid of that freeloader?" Paddy then leans in. "You know, *you* can do better."

"Where's the better? I sure as hell haven't seen any."

He is about to say something when a chorus of loud voices bursts through the door.

The Americans.

All eyes turn to them. Two women enter wearing bright jackets and looking remarkably alike in their short blonde hair and blue eyes. There are two men with them. The tall, lanky man has dark, shiny hair pulled back into a ponytail. The other one, stout with pocked skin and a stomach protruding over low-slung trousers, says, "Is that bacon I smell?" He looks around. Spying the stove, he squeals, "Oh look, it's that peat stuff burning. Cool."

Fiona jumps to her feet and follows them to the bar. "Hallo," she says mostly to the ponytailed American. He just grins with teeth brighter than any I've ever seen. She whispers to me, "Yummy."

Paddy bellows, "A fine welcome to Paddy's Pub." He motions to the men on the stools to move aside. They grunt, but move to a table.

Striding up to the bar, the women coo, "What should we get?" The pudgy American says, "You're *supposed* to get Guinness." Turning to Paddy, he pulls out his wallet. "A round, please."

"Half pints for the ladies and pints for the lads?" Paddy starts pouring the pints. Fiona runs her manicured nails through her short-cropped brown hair. Her jacket opens, revealing her low cut sweater.

"Naw, make them all pints." He whips out his money and turns to his friends. "It's cheaper than two half pints." The women nod, but the ponytailed man's dark eyes linger on Fiona.

The Americans share their story, similar to ones we hear each year when the students arrive from Minnesota to stay in the cottages for the semester. It's their first time abroad, and they want to see the Emerald Island and experience new people and a new culture.

Paddy boasts about the dances he will start next weekend. Just for them. The short guy buying the drinks tells us that he is Henry. The one with the ponytail is Tom. They ask where they can get some food at this hour, as nothing is open that they could see while walking through town.

"I know just the place," Fiona says. "There's a chipper in Westport. And a great pub nearby with fantastic music." She grabs her bag and buttons her jacket. "I'll drive."

"I read about fish and chips in the guidebook." Henry drains his beer. "Awesome."

Fiona leads the Americans out. For only a moment, I debate whether to just go home.

There must be more than this. The thought of entertaining the Americans as we do each year has lost its appeal. They will stay for three months and then leave. I will still be here. Mikey will still try to get in my pants until he finds someone better. Maeve will still try to get Bobby to come home and be with her and the kids instead of staying at the pub until closing time. Da will still drink, fish, and pretend he's working when he's not on his stool talking to Paddy. I will still be working for Granda and saving my money to do nothing in particular.

The thought of being home alone suffocates me. I grab my coat and follow Fiona and the Americans.

As I walk out of Paddy's, I nearly run into Da, who's on his way in. Earlier in the day, we made small talk as we got the Americans settled, and we tried to figure out something to eat. He now asks if I'll be home later. This is the first time he's asked me this. I just shrug and catch up with Fiona.

When my phone rings the next morning, I'm buried under the blanket, still in my clothes. I don't remember getting into bed. I vaguely remember the fish and chips and the chatty Americans. My phone is on the chair across the room. I grab the phone just before the call goes into voicemail.

"Do you have my bra?" Fiona's voice croaks in my ear.

"Why would I have your bra?" I mutter, slipping back under the warm covers. The sun looks fully up.

"Well, I seem to have come home without it. Or misplaced it. I thought you might know."

"How unfortunate. They can be quite expensive. You really should keep better care of your undergarments."

"You don't need to be so cheeky." Fiona's voice has the whiney tone she uses to get what she wants.

"Sorry. My head feels like it's going to explode." I grab a pillow and put it over my face. The room spins. I flip the pillow and feel the coolness on my cheek. My stomach lurches. "I'll call you back."

I barely make it to the bathroom before vomiting. Some hits the toilet. Some hits the floor. Some hits my sweater. It tastes foul. I rest my head on the cool porcelain tub.

"Need a little hair of the dog?"

Da is standing in the door in his waders and flannel shirt. As he holds out a chipped cup and saucer, his hand shakes.

I groan and put my head down.

"Heard you come in. That Fiona knows how to make those tires squeal." When I don't say anything, he says, "Paddy's fit to be tied that you took the Americans somewhere else instead of patronizing his fine establishment."

"He'll get over it." The room stops spinning, but I'm afraid to move for fear it will start again.

"Aye, he will." Da doesn't leave. He just looks at me. Then he scrunches his face and asks, "Aren't you supposed to be training?"

I close my eyes and mutter, "You giving me advice?"

"No. Just a message." He digs in his pocket and pulls out a piece of paper. "Doc's son, Ryan, called this morning. I wrote his number down here. He said he has your scarf."

Chapter Eight

The things I have done with Fiona. You'd think I'd learn.

I can't even remember what Doc's son looks like. I remember he's young and I remember his strength as he carried Ma from the car. He saved her. The last thing I want to do is call him.

I stagger back to my bed. Pulling the covers over my head, I curl into a ball. When I was a wee girl, Ma used to come into my room and rub my hair and my back when I was sick. She'd sing songs that she couldn't remember the full lyrics to. It didn't matter. I'd fall asleep, and later, I'd feel better.

Da hollers, "I'm going to Galway with Paddy to get some new gear. Can you manage?"

I groan, "Yeah. I'm fine." Rolling over, I look at the clock. It's nearly noon.

When I wake again, it's only because the home phone is ringing. It's nearly two o'clock now. I scramble to the wall-mounted phone in the kitchen. My voice croaks when I answer.

"Eliza." It's Mr. Walters. "I was wondering if you'd like to come over for tea today. That is, if you have time."

"Okay, but I have to get a run in first."

"Ah, yes. I heard you were doing the Tri-Burgh triathlon in June. How's the training going?"

"Excellent," I lie.

"Come by after four. Johnny and I will go on our bike ride and be back by then."

I agree to stop by, then hang up.

While the thought of running curdles my stomach, I remind myself that I deserve this. I'm about to get ready to go out when I see Ryan's name and number scrawled on the back of an envelope.

I call Ryan's number hoping for voicemail, but he answers. I stammer, immediately self-conscious of my voice and what might have happened last night. "Hallo, this is Eliza Conroy. You…"

"How nice of you to ring back." It sounds like he's outside in the wind.

"Um, Da said you called and have my scarf."

"You left it in the pub." He begs my pardon and talks to someone. When he returns, he says, "I would love to see you again. Maybe finish where we left off? Dinner tonight around eight at Dunning's?

"Grand." I try to sound perky.

"I don't think I've met anyone quite like your friend Fiona," Ryan says.

"She's one of a kind," I say.

"I almost pissed my pants when she took off her bra, stood on the table, and yelled, 'Going to the top bidder!'"

"Fiona can get gee-eyed after too many."

Ryan laughs. "The tubby American was dense to pay that much, if you ask me, but he seemed pleased with himself when he wore it on his head." He pauses. "It was unexpected."

He has no idea.

After we confirm the plans to meet and say goodbye, I collapse my head in my hands and try to remember anything from last night.

~

Instead of my usual path along Clew Bay and then to the river, I take the road into town. With the wind to my back, past rock fences and grazing sheep, I focus on putting each foot in front of the other. Too early in the season for tourists; there are only a few cars that pass me. It's flat. Even so, my breathing is labored.

My legs, still tight, carry me along the sidewalk lined with empty kegs. I wave at Fiona's mother sweeping the sidewalk in front of the grocery store. Even though I'd love to stop, I keep running. Fiona's car is taking two spots. Drapes remain drawn in her family's home above the store.

I end up walking on the way back, clutching my side. The run never got easy.

The breeze off the water is warm and salty, like the tears I've shed the past days. The bump on my head is down, but my head throbs from too many pints. Looking down, I see a patch of dandelions. Da calls them "piss in the beds." Ma said they were her favorite flowers. I'd pick bouquets of dandelions and put them in a juice glass. When they wilted too soon, I'd cry.

My throat constricts and it's hard to see the road. I stumble on a rock and nearly fall.

~

Shortly after four o'clock I walk up to Mr. Walters's door, past the three-wheeled bike parked under the four-paned windows. He answers in a frayed cardigan sweater.

"Come in. Come in." He swings the door wide open. Inside, I smell cinnamon. On the table, there is a pan of Irish bread pudding and a plate of cucumber sandwiches. The table is neatly set for two with place mats and cloth napkins.

Johnny jumps on my leg until I bend down to pet him and then he licks my hand. Mr. Walters hobbles to the table, pulls out a chair, and motions for me to sit.

"Help yourself while I get the tea."

Sitting down, I look around. I've never been in a former teacher's house. The living room has more furniture than fits comfortably. It smells like the windows haven't been opened much over the years. Stacks of papers clutter the end tables and upright piano in the far corner. He pours me tea and adds milk. I don't tell him that I drink it black.

"So, Eliza. I imagine this is most distressing and quite a shock." He pushes the plate of sandwiches toward me. They are cut into squares with their crusts removed.

I take one and sip my tea. It's lukewarm and bitter, even with milk. I don't see a sugar bowl on the table.

"Any news?" He peers at me over his thick glasses and filmy blue eyes. "Have you talked to her?"

"No. She won't see me. Or Da." I look down at the sandwich and focus on chewing until it dissolves. As I do, I can feel him looking at me.

Sighing, Mr. Walters says, "I suppose she has her reasons, but..." He pauses and looks out the window at the dimming sky. "I've known her since she was a wee girl and always worried about her."

I stop chewing. "Why?"

"Oh, she was different." He closes his eyes and says, "I'll never forget her beautiful voice."

I scrunch my forehead.

Mr. Walters looks at me kindly. "You didn't know? Well, she was self-conscious, perhaps." He scoops out some pudding onto a delicate china plate and slides it towards me. "Do *you* sing?"

"Hell, no! Oh, sorry. I..." I can feel my face flush.

"It's fine, dear." He laughs, which was something I never heard him do as a teacher. "Other than the eyes, you don't resemble her."

"We don't have much in common," I mutter and take a bite of the pudding. It doesn't taste anything like the kind Ma made. Too dry. Too sweet. A lump forms in my throat. My eyes swell with tears. Blinking, I try to stop them, but they flow down my face. I wipe them away with my sleeve without putting down the spoon. They don't stop.

Mr. Walters scoots his chair closer. Digging in his pocket, he pulls out a monogrammed linen handkerchief and hands it to me. I can smell the cigar smoke embedded in his wool sweater.

Sobs convulse my body.

I haven't cried this hard. Ever. Not even when I found Ma.

Eventually I pull myself together, apologize, and tell him that I have to get going. Mr. Walters has a sad expression on his craggy face. The dog wags his tail and follows me to the door.

As I'm leaving, Mr. Walters says, "You're always welcome here, Eliza. Johnny and I always like company."

It's half past eight and there's no sign of Ryan McCullough at Dunning's. I crane my head toward the door as people walk in. No one looks familiar. The waitress refills my Diet Coke and asks if I want to order. When I shake my head, she looks at me in a pathetic, knowing way. I keep pulling out my phone, looking for a text message from him even though I've never given him my number. It's something to do.

Finally at nine o'clock I pay the tab and leave. I just want the day to be over.

It isn't until I'm nearly at Louisburgh that I notice the car behind me. It flashes its bright lights and follows closely, turning when I turn. When I reach our cottage and stop, it pulls in beside me. I don't recognize either the car or the person getting out.

Then I do. It's the vet who saved Ma.

Ryan McCullough walks toward me, looking smart in his jeans and leather jacket. "You probably want to give it to me for standing you up."

"It's fine." My tone is too sweet, too casual. I notice we are the same height.

There is no moon or even stars to cut the darkness. "I can't believe I didn't think to get your number. There was an emergency at the clinic. Then I had to go home and change."

"Don't worry about it," I say.

We stand awkwardly near my car. Cool air blows my loose-hanging hair. I brush a strand away and pull my jacket in tighter.

"I got there just as you were leaving and tried yelling, but you didn't hear me." He stands a few feet away, holding my scarf. I hold my hand out.

Ryan hands me the scarf and says, "I don't suppose you want to go get something to eat now?"

I shake my head. "It's been a long day."

He looks toward the cottage with an impish smile. "I promise not to stay long."

I invite him in, and we walk to the door. It's dark inside except for the glow of a smoldering fire. After flipping on the light, I walk to the fireplace and toss on more peat. Wind rattles the panes. I close the drapes and move Da's tackle box from the table. "Have a seat."

"This is so quaint." Ryan walks toward the fireplace and warms his hands.

I roll my eyes and head into the kitchen. Dirty dishes are piled in the sink. Peering into the fridge, I say, "I have Diet Coke if you'd rather that over tea, but not much else."

"Tea's grand."

Ryan looks at the scattered pictures. "Love your hair, especially in this picture where it's sticking straight up." Then he sits on the overstuffed couch and, with his arm stretched over the top, he looks back at me. His cowlick highlights his boyish face.

When I hand him the cup and saucer, Ryan says, "Your friend is quite the spark plug."

"She's that." I sit on the chair opposite him.

"I was hoping we could talk. Especially after our dance." He sips his tea. "I'm afraid I was a bit taken aback when you kissed me."

I gasp.

"You don't remember it, do you?"

I cover my eyes with my hands. "Shite. I made an arse of myself."

"Nothing else happened, if that's what you're wondering. I wasn't that daft to realize you might not be yourself. I wanted to bring your scarf back and check in. Just to make sure you're alright."

I can't think of anything to say, but think a dark hole to fall into right about now would be nice.

The only sound is the wind. Ryan breaks the silence. "So tell me about yourself—something I don't know about you. Did you go to university?"

I shake my head. "No. Maybe someday. Right now I just help my granda run the B&B. He owns these holiday cottages, too."

"Sounds fun."

"Not really, but it's money. What do you do when you're not working?"

"Well, you heard me play my guitar at O'Grady's last night. My mates talked me into joining them years ago. It's good fun, good *craic*. Other than that, I'm an outdoor nut. Bike, run, surf. You name it. If there's a race, I do it."

"I'm doing the Tri-Burgh this year. First time."

"Really? How's training?"

When I tell him that I have started, he pounds me with questions about my program. How many miles do I run each day? What strength training program am I following? What cross training regime has worked best?

I tell him that I run, but haven't given much mind to the other things. Not yet.

He says matter-of-factly, "I hope you won't take this wrong, but what you put into your body is as important as the miles you log. You probably should watch the drink." He reaches for his tea that he set down when we started talking about training. He adds, "If you're serious."

I feel my body stiffen. "You just saw me on a bad night."

"Don't get me wrong. I drink every now and then. I'm just saying that if you're serious about training, like you say you are, then every pint will set you back. That's all."

I want to throw my cup of tea at him. "After everything, I just wanted some craic."

"Oh, please don't think I'm judging you. I want to help. Maybe we could even do a run or ride together sometime?"

"Maybe. Obviously I need to start training."

My sarcasm isn't lost on him. He slaps his leg and tells me he has to get back to Westport. Before he leaves, he asks me for my email address. He tells me that he will email the training programs that we talked about. I scribble it on a piece of paper. Neither of us asks the other for a cell number.

We walk to his car, making small talk about the weather. Then I watch his taillights fade away.

Chapter Nine

The morning sun glows low on the horizon as I run. A light breeze carries birdsongs. My labored breath produces puffs of vapor. My legs barely lift off the ground. They feel like steel girders as I wind through the gently rolling hills. Still, I don't stop.

Ryan's words still sting. I want to prove him wrong: People can have craic every now and then and still compete. I run faster, pushing through the pain.

When I get back home, drenched and exhausted, it's quiet inside. I fill a glass with water, guzzle it down, and open all the drapes.

There's no sign of Da. His bedroom door is closed. I listen for his snores, but don't hear any.

In the freezer is some blood sausage that I defrost and start boiling. I peel and slice a few potatoes and begin frying them with onions. The steam condenses on the kitchen window. In a bowl, I crack eggs and whisk. I grab two plates and silverware. I holler for Da to come eat.

He doesn't answer.

I dump the water from the sausages and begin browning them. Into a well-buttered frying pan, I slide the eggs, sprinkle them with salt and pepper, and turn the burner up.

The kitchen smells like Sunday mornings and Ma's cooking. Except it's Monday, and Ma is not here.

I holler for Da again. Still no answer.

Silence answers when I rap on the door. When I open the door, I see the bed is unmade. Clothes are strewn on the floor and heaped on the chair closest to Ma's side of the bed. The drapes are open. He hasn't come home.

In the kitchen, I look for a note but find none. I call him, but it goes straight into voicemail. I hang up without leaving a message.

Sitting at the table, I eat my breakfast and stare out the window toward Clew Bay. I wonder what Ma's doing right now and if she thinks about me. The food sits heavy in my stomach. I scrape most of it into the rubbish bin.

I get my laptop from my bedroom and power it up. Logging into my email, I think for a moment that Ma might have sent me a message even though she rarely uses a computer.

Ryan's email is the first one I see. He writes how nice it was to see me and suggests that we meet for a run this coming Saturday as he will be in Louisburgh visiting his uncle. I can't believe it when I read his uncle is Mr. Walters. He attached three different training programs: novice, intermediate, and advanced. Even under the novice program, I'm behind schedule. Way behind. I hesitate, but reply that would be fun.

Fun? Who am I kidding?

When I go to town a short time later, the sun has slunk beneath grey, stacked clouds. A light mist is falling. Outside his pub, Paddy is unloading full kegs from a truck, hoisting them overhead without effort. He doesn't notice me until I am a foot away and say, "Hey."

He puts the keg down. "You're out and about early."

"Yeah. Seen Da?"

Paddy motions to his flat above the bar. "On the couch."

Even though I know the answer, I say, "All night?"

"Aye. Fell asleep on his stool. Didn't make sense to send him home in that condition, so I hauled his sorry arse upstairs. You can go rile him."

"Why would I do that?"

Paddy shrugs and goes back to unloading. I lean against the peeling paint of the pub's facade, feel the mist on my face, and watch Paddy work.

"There's something I've been wondering about," I say. "It's about Ma and Da."

"What about them?"

"You've known them both a long time."

"'Tis true." He laughs and wipes his forehead. "Too long now."

"Are they happy?" I ask.

"Why the hell would you ask me such a thing?" Paddy says.

"Just wondering."

"They're like every other married couple. Sometimes they get along. Sometimes they don't."

There is no breeze, just the heavy, moist air. Only a few cars are parked along the street. Most stores are still closed. In the distance, the bells from St. Patrick's Church summon the few people, mostly elderly, who attend daily mass.

I say, "She left her wedding ring on the windowsill in the kitchen."

He scoffs. "So?"

"She never took it off."

52

"People do things that surprise us." Paddy rubs the stubble on his rugged, slightly lined face. "I wouldn't read too much into it." He goes back to unloading the kegs.

In a soft voice, I ask, "Does Da love her?"

He stops. "What kind of question is that? Hell, he married her, didn't he?"

"I saw their wedding picture. Just the three of you were there. In Dublin, of all places," I say. "Why was that?"

"You're full of questions all of a sudden. Why ask me?"

"You're the only one here right now."

Paddy shakes his head and rests his arm on the side of the truck. "Your granda never liked Seamus. No one was good enough for his little Annie. He never even let her date. Not that she seemed inclined."

"So they hid it from Granda?"

"It wasn't a long courtship. Pissed your granda off when he found out." A car with no muffler roars past us and turns toward Westport. Smoke trails from the tailpipe. Paddy watches the car until it disappears. Then, with a lowered voice, he says, "Madder still when he found out she was pregnant. Wouldn't go to the wedding."

"She was *pregnant* when she got married?"

"Math not your strong suit?" This time his eyes didn't twinkle like they usually did when he teased me.

Ma always said I was big and strong for a premature baby. I say, "Did he want to marry her? Did he love her?"

"Jaysus, Eliza. Ask *him*." Paddy heaves a full keg over his shoulder and walks inside, letting the door slam shut.

It never dawned on me to question Ma.

I'm about to follow Paddy when the group of Americans who went to Westport with us on Saturday come out of the chemist. They wave. The dumpy one, Henry, walks toward me. I plant a smile and cross, meeting him in the middle of the street.

Henry's pocked face lights up. "I've been looking for Fiona, but can't find her. Do you know how I can get ahold of her?"

I try to look surprised. "Sometimes she helps her parents in the grocery. Maybe she's there?"

"I checked. She's not."

"Oh. Well, she may have gone to Galway or Castlebar shopping. I'm sure you'll see her at the disco this weekend."

His face falls. "We have to take the bus on Friday to Sligo. Or Cork. Somewhere. I can't remember. We're gone all weekend checking out some old churches and castles."

"That's too bad. Paddy will be disappointed. He had everything planned."

The others join us. The girls smile and say hello; the ponytailed boy looks bored. They tell me everything they've seen in town. It's not much. No one mentions our time in Westport. Another group of American students, walking on the other side of the street, calls their names. I agree to tell Fiona that Henry's looking for her. They join their friends and walk back toward the cottages.

I dig my phone out of my pocket and push the number I programmed for St. Patrick's Hospital in Dublin. After a long wait, the person on the line confirms that Ma won't take calls or visitors. Then the line goes dead after the person wishes me a fine day.

Chapter Ten

After getting Ryan's email and the training plans, I'd emailed him that a run would be excellent. Luckily he had a conflict, and we pushed our run out another week. Now, two weeks since I last saw him, I'm in a better place. I've followed the intermediate plan religiously, eaten better and avoided the drink. Not a drop has passed my lips.

My old legs are back. I feel more like myself. I'm strong. But logging the running miles in the training plan humbles me. Humiliates might be the better word. Luckily the triathlon isn't for months. Running is my best leg. Next month I will focus more on the swimming and biking.

You would have thought that I flung the Holy Bible in Clew Bay and spit on the Pope himself if you talked to Fiona these past two weeks. She never stops reminding me how abandoned she feels. Still, I run. Still, I stay out of the pubs.

Da and I continue to avoid each other. Actually, I avoid everyone. It's easier.

For too long, I've been spinning, lost and out of control. Running, alone in my thoughts, I can control where my feet land. Not the lies. Not Ma and the fact she doesn't want to see me. Not Da and the fact that he can't go without the drink and doesn't want to come home. It is just my legs pounding the ground. In wide-open space, I'm free. My head finally clears.

I've tried to explain this to Fiona. She used to listen. She used to care. Or maybe I never noticed that she didn't.

Today I'm meeting Ryan at Mr. Walters's for an afternoon run. As I sit on a chair in the living room and lace my runners, Fiona stretches on the couch like a cat in the midday sun. She stopped late this morning after her mother told her she wasn't needed to work at the grocery store. Her half-opened eyes are cushioned in puffy bags. She says, "Tell me again why you're meeting him."

"I told you. He's done all sorts of races and triathlons."

"First he saves your Ma's life. Now he's your personal coach." Fiona sits up, her red eyes wide. "Is he yummy?"

"Christ, Fiona."

"Just asking. Maybe I should come with you. I'm sure Weird Willie would love to see me." Fiona tosses her head back against the faded couch and laughs. "I think I had more detentions than anyone else in his class."

"You never shut your big mouth."

"We all aren't as perfect as you, Miss Priss. You used to be at least a little fun."

"I'm just off the drink while I train. Lay off!"

"Fun was better. Now you're just a dry shite." Fiona admires her painted nails. "You might want to know that I met two men in Westport last night. From Montana in the States. *Real men.* Not students."

"So?"

"So I'm taking them to Galway tonight. You should come." She looks like a child excited for Christmas morning. "One for each of us."

"No." I stand up and lift my wind trousers and jacket from the hooks near the door. In the mirror hanging on the wall, I catch my reflection. My long hair frames my face. My skin is clear and my eyes look bright. I finally look rested.

"They're here for three weeks," Fiona says. "I've promised them a good time."

"You always deliver." The plastic trousers crinkle as I slip them over my running tights.

"*Please*? You can have your pick." Fiona does her best pout and flutters her long lashes.

I walk over to the chair across from Fiona, sit down, and pull my hair back into a ponytail. "I pick staying home."

Fiona's phone rings. It's in her bag near the door. She scrambles to get up. Her foot, tucked under the cushion, flips it over when she hurtles over the back of the couch. The cushion lands on the floor while Fiona lands on her feet. She digs through her bag. Breathlessly, Fiona answers it. She looks over at me and mouths, "It's them."

As she talks, Fiona checks her face in the mirror. She pushes her short hair in different directions until she settles on how it looks best and then admires herself fully. A tourist once said she looked right out of a trendy magazine with her chic haircut and stylish clothes. She never let me forget that. No one ever said that about me.

"No. It's only going to be me." Fiona casts a look at me and says to whomever is on the phone, "My *friend* is deserting us. But I'll see you soon."

Fiona hangs up and snatches her leather jacket off the back of the couch. She heads toward the door. Her sweet perfume trails her. Then she stops and says, "You are getting so dull." In a huff, she walks out, leaving the door open. The cool, salty air wafts in.

I reach over to replace the threadbare cushion that Fiona knocked off. It smells like peat and wet dog even though we've never had a dog. There's lint, a few coins, and a couple of ballpoint pens scattered on the sagging, ripped lining of the couch. I swipe my hand across it to collect them. My hand hits something hard under the lining. Digging my hand under it, I pull out a book with gold embossed lettering: Journal. My fingers brush the lettering like a feather floating on air.

Opening the cover, I see Ma's writing.

I never knew she kept a journal. Usually she sat at the kitchen table staring out the window, not writing in a book on the couch. She rarely read or even watched the television. Or if she did, I never noticed.

The cover of the journal is smooth, soft leather. It feels like velvet. I bring it to my nose. It smells like Ma. She sometimes wears the Lily eau de toilette that I ordered online from Crabtree & Evelyn. I get her a new bottle every year for Christmas. Last year, I also gave her Lily body lotion and shower gel.

The journal is only half-filled. I turn to the first entry. It's written nearly fifteen years ago. In Ma's perfect penmanship, she wrote, "He gets mad and says I baby her. I watch her sleep and know I can't protect her. I can't be there all the time. It kills me." My throat tightens.

The wind slams the door shut. I jump. The sun has dipped behind a cloud, casting shadows in the room. I shudder, curl up on the couch, and stare at the small, perfect writing. It almost looks like calligraphy.

I remember when Da said I was old enough to sleep alone. I was five. Most nights, Ma curled up next to me in her flannel nightgown. Usually she smelled sweet, especially if she had been baking, but sometimes she smelled more like bleach. She stroked my hair until I fell asleep. I'd wake alone most nights, except when Da didn't come home. Then Ma stayed all night. Ma eventually stopped coming in, although I can't remember when that was.

Ma didn't write every day. When she did, it was mostly about me, Fiona, and things I was doing in school. It was cryptic. Things I wanted to forget—my first period, my first bout with acne.

I start flipping through the pages. Most of it is dull, like her lists of things to do and the price of things at the grocer. Some entries don't make much sense. There are large gaps in time. Ma's writing starts to get sloppy and the entries are no longer dated.

The room grows brighter as sun streams through the lace curtains. One minute it looks like rain, and then the sun comes out. Always unpredictable.

I'm about to close the book when I see an undated entry: "He said it was over. I now know it's not. He doesn't think I know."

The next page there is one last, undated entry: "It's time."

The rest of the pages are blank.

Was this written on the morning I found her? Was she sitting on the couch writing it while waiting for me to call or come home? All of a sudden, the image of Ma in the tub flashes in front of me. A lump in my throat prevents me from swallowing.

It's absurd to think Da is having an affair. My head swims

in questions. Who'd want him? Wouldn't I know? Someone would talk. Even Paddy couldn't keep that quiet. Certainly Maeve would fall over herself to tell me.

My phone buzzes. It's Ryan. He's at Mr. Walters's house and ready to run whenever I am.

~

I slip on my thin gloves and step outside. There is a slight breeze. The sun ducks behind scattered clouds, then reemerges. Without stretching, I start running the short distance to town.

Slowly, my legs loosen.

Outside Mr. Walters's house, Ryan is stretching against his Subaru with the rear-mounted bike rack. There's a Yakima rack on top. He waves when he sees me and smiles broadly. "Lovely to see you." He adjusts the straps of a hydration pack slipped over his shoulders. "I hope you're ready for a good workout. I thought we could even do some off-trail running once we get warmed up." He puts on a baseball cap that conceals his cowlick and highlights his freckled, boyish face. "From your email, it sounds like training's right on schedule."

"More or less." I've forgotten to bring a water bottle, but don't want to go back to the cottage. "Lead the way."

The pace is manageable—even easy—when we start out side by side.

We make small talk about races he's done and won, and races I hope to do after the one in June. He's a wealth of information. I just listen as he floods me with training tips.

We take the route away from Clew Bay toward Westport, past the rocky fields, stone fences, and painted sheep.

He doesn't ask about Ma. I'm relieved. I try to think only of where my feet land and how my breath feels. We settle into a rhythm. The wind from the west propels us forward. My breath, originally labored, is now even.

The sun dips beneath heavy, dark clouds. We have run nearly seven miles when Ryan points ahead to Croagh Patrick. "How about hill training on the Reek?"

My legs are tightening and the last thing I want to do is run up the rocky, uneven path, but I try to sound enthusiastic as I say, "Sure. Why not?"

This year I haven't walked, let alone run, the 762 meter mountain named after St. Patrick. I'm hoping he's not planning to go to the top, but I don't tell him this.

We reach the base and start the steady climb. Ryan, leading the way, runs like a gazelle. His feet look like they are floating over the embedded stones. With his jaw set, he looks up. I'm a different story. Clumsy and slow, I look down, watching where my feet land.

Fat raindrops splat my face. I pull up my windbreaker's hood and try to cover some of my face. I yell to Ryan, "What's the plan?"

"How about to that next point and then turn around?" The incline has become steeper and rockier. "That okay with you?"

"Yeah." I zip my jacket and plow forward. My legs burn.

Glancing behind at Clew Bay, I see a grey sheet shrouding the smattering of islands normally visible from this height. The wind slaps my face. Ryan has turned around. He's at my side with his eyes squinted. We turn back and run downhill, side by side, into the wind. Thunder claps. Sheets of rain pelt our faces. The wind, once at our backs, now restrains us from the front like an invisible hand.

I can barely see in front of me. Ryan speeds up and leads the way. We are single file going down the steep path.

I try to keep up. My feet propel me forward. I try to slow down. The rocks are slippery. I try to avoid them. The wind blinds me. I put my head down, looking only where each foot lands.

We are nearly at the base. I look up through the rain. Almost there. I can see the road. A car blurs by.

Suddenly, my foot slides off a large rock. My ankle twists. Then snaps. I try catching myself, but can't. Rolling down the rocks, I almost plow Ryan over. My head strikes rocks. Blood seeps down my face and into my mouth. My screams echo in my head. I land, unable to move.

Ryan comes to my side. Leaning down, he looks at my ankle. Writhing, I can't speak. His face tells me what I already know. It's broken.

Ryan digs out his phone from his zippered pocket, turns so the wind is at his back. I hear him tell someone to bring his car to the base of Croagh Patrick. Then he stuffs the phone back and says, "We've got to get to the road." He slides his arm under me and lifts me up. I cry out.

The wind is now a full gale. Rain cuts across my face. I lean into Ryan's chest. He holds me closer as he navigates down the mountain.

By the time we make it to the road, Mr. Walters is there with Ryan's car.

Ryan opens the rear door and slides me into the leather seat. I try not to scream in pain, but can't help it. I watch the wipers beat furiously as the rain pounds the windshield. Tears cascade down my wind-chafed cheeks all the way to the hospital in Castlebar.

Chapter Eleven

Surgery is the only option, the doctor finally tells me after a long wait in the emergency room. When I wake up the next day, I am alone.

Outside my darkened room, carts rattle down the hall and unfamiliar voices pass by. My nurse's name is scrawled across a whiteboard on the wall next to the mounted television. I have no idea who she is. Or where she is. On a narrow, moveable table sits an insulated pitcher and a glass. Next to it is a tray with a covered plate, orange juice secured in plastic wrap, and a pot of tea. It's just out of my reach.

My immobilized foot throbs. I try to sit, but pain shoots up my leg. I sink back onto the flat pillow. I shiver and pull the thin blanket up over my faded hospital gown.

Ryan walks through the door. He's carrying a stuffed bear and a bouquet of yellow tulips.

"You're awake." He puts the flowers down on the table near the head of the bed and hands me the bear. "To keep you company." He smiles, waiting for me to say something. He's wearing jeans and a mock turtleneck under his waterproof jacket.

"Thanks." I force a smile and take his gift store bear. I let it fall at my side. My head feels cloudy, and I want to close my eyes.

"I feel terrible about what happened," he says. "I should have gotten us down the mountain sooner."

I shrug. It's difficult swallowing. I lick my sandpaper lips. Ryan picks up the plastic glass and pours water into it. He unwraps a straw and sticks it in. "Drink this." He holds the glass to my mouth. The water is lukewarm. Some trickles out of the corner of my mouth. Even my arm, bruised and hooked to an IV, feels like someone else's. I can barely move it as I wipe the water from my mouth. A gauze bandage covers my forehead where I hit my head on the rocks. My palms are red and scraped.

Ryan paces with a worried look on his face. "It seemed so perfect." I can tell he's mulling over each part of the run, wondering when he missed the clue to go back.

"Does Da know?"

He shakes his head. "Willie's trying to reach him. Apparently he's still in Dublin."

"Why?" I close my eyes and try to think. "I need to call him. Or Fiona." It dawns on me that I didn't bring my phone running. I try sitting up. "My phone's at home."

"We can get it when you're discharged."

"When's that?"

"Depends on what the surgeon says."

As if on cue, a portly man with a shiny head strides into the room. "Good morning. I'm Dr. O'Toole." Lifting the blanket, he looks at my ankle. "It looks good. Well, maybe not to you, but I do fine work." He laughs, amused with himself, and comes to the head of the bed. I don't smile. His face fades to a frown. "Nasty break. There are pins in it to hold it in place."

"When can I go home?"

"Today. You can lie there with your foot elevated as well as you can here. You'll need crutches."

Ryan comes closer. "I have some she can use."

"And someone there with you."

"There will be," Ryan says.

"Excellent." Dr. O'Toole flips through papers. "The nurse will come and explain what you need to know in terms of proper care when you're home, medications, and follow-up instructions." He pats my arm like someone acknowledging a loyal dog, and then excuses himself when I say I don't have any questions.

I feel numb, like I'm floating in a dream. I close my eyes. I imagine myself outside, free to go where my feet take me, over the squishy bog, the uneven pastures, and the gravel road. I imagine the wind and misty air on my face.

The familiar cigar scent wakes me. Mr. Walters is sitting in the chair next to Ryan with his arms crossed over his protruding stomach. He's not wearing a hat. His sparse grey hair is combed over to the side. They are whispering with serious faces.

Ryan spies my open eyes and says, "We were wondering if you were going to sleep the day away. The nurse has been waiting for you to wake up."

I clear my throat. "Sorry."

Mr. Walters hoists himself up and comes over. "Nothing to be sorry about, my dear." He rests his thick fingers on the metal bedrail, arches his eyebrows and says, "You poor thing."

I say, "Can I go home now?" Ryan exchanges a look with Mr. Walters. I look to each of them. "What?"

"Your father is going to be in Dublin a little longer," Mr. Walters says. "Paddy told me he's dealing with matters pertaining to your mother."

I try to sit up, but am able only to lean back on my elbows. "What happened? Is she okay?"

"She's fine." Mr. Walters pats my shoulder. I can smell his Old Spice aftershave. "Paddy tells me your mother wanted to see Seamus, but she's not coming home. Not yet."

"When will he be back?" My voice sounds croaky and desperate.

Mr. Walters sighs. "Who knows? They have things to work out." He pushes aside a long strand of my hair that has slipped across my face.

Ryan steps forward. "The plan is that you will go to Willie's. Just until your da gets home. I'll get the crutches and stay the night to make sure you're okay with the meds and the swelling."

"I want to go home."

"There is no other option," Mr. Walters says. "Paddy's steps are unmanageable. And your grandparents are on holiday. You can't stay alone."

"Fiona could come over." I look to Ryan, but he just shrugs and looks at his uncle.

Mr. Walters laughs. "Really, my dear. We could never leave you alone with her. Who knows what state she'd be in by morning, or who she'd bring with her? During the last few days, two strange men have been at her side."

"I want to go home." My voice sounds small.

"Just one night," Ryan says. "Your da might be home by tomorrow."

If there's a choice, I don't see it.

⟋⟋⟋

After I am finally discharged, Ryan drives me to Mr. Walters's house. The sky is darkening, and the pain medication is wearing off. My foot, now wrapped, burns. An empty, hollow feeling in my stomach reminds me that I haven't eaten much besides saltines, but the thought of food gags me.

Mr. Walters greets us at the door, "Come in. Come in." He spreads his arms wide and steps aside so we can get by.

The pads of the crutches dig into my armpits. I try putting my weight on my scuffed hands, rather than the pits, to hold myself up—just as the nurse showed me—but it proves more difficult than I thought. With much effort, I hobble a few steps. Then I need to stop and catch my breath. No one says anything. They just watch, avoiding my eyes. They wait until I make it inside.

There's a fire in the hearth and the smell of fried potatoes and lamb. Johnny jumps on me. I teeter slightly. Mr. Walters yells at him to get down and go to his bed, which he does.

"Dinner isn't quite ready," Mr. Walters says. "Make yourself at home and comfortable until then." He goes into the kitchen and stirs something on the stove.

Ryan stays right behind me and lightly touches my back, steadying me. "It's high time you get that ankle up. The spare room is the first door on the right." He points to the hallway off the living room.

With each step forward, I grimace. I'm careful not to touch down my foot, but searing pain in my ankle shoots up my leg. It feels like nothing I've experienced. Burning. An electrical surging. Pulsating fire. I don't know how much longer I can hold back the tears.

Ryan helps me onto the bed. He puts two pillows under my ankle and tosses an afghan over my legs. I lean back. My breath, high in my chest, comes out in soundless bursts. Ryan brings over another pillow and tucks it under my head. It smells musty. I sneeze, jolting my body. I gasp at the excruciating pain.

"Let's get you some pain meds." Ryan sits down beside me on the bed and pulls out the prescription we'd picked up. He unscrews the child-resistant cap and hands me two pills and a water bottle that he takes from his backpack.

I take a sip. The pills catch in my throat. I drink more water and hand the bottle back to him. "Thanks," I say, collapsing onto the pillows.

A small lamp on the nightstand casts a glow in the sparse room. Only one wall has something on it: a crucifix. Heavy drapes cover the small window on the far wall. Ryan touches my forehead with his cool hand. Then, his slender fingers comb my hair away from my face. I close my eyes. I can't help it. Then I reopen them. He doesn't stop. Softly, he starts humming. It's a familiar tune that I can't place. The pain ebbs. My body sinks into the soft mattress. My eyes flutter. I try to keep them open, but they are heavy. My breath rises from my belly and escapes from my half opened mouth as he strokes my hair and hums.

I pretend I'm in my own bed and that it's my mother's

hand stroking my hair. I let my lids close and drift into dreamless sleep.

———

Pain wakes me. The light remains on, but there's no sound in the other room. My pills are on the table along with a note from Ryan: "You needed the sleep so we didn't wake you for dinner. Holler when you wake up and I can help." He wrote out the schedule for the medication and left his running watch next to a full glass of water. It's three o'clock in the morning, past the time to take the pills.

After taking the medicine, I lie back and stare at the walls and wish I were in my own bed.

I replay everything that has happened in the last weeks. I'm here with people that I don't know, and I can't even get up to use the bathroom by myself.

Time passes. I keep looking through the slit in the drapes for a sign that the sun is coming up.

I cry soundless tears.

Looking around, I don't see any tissue. I reach over and open the drawer of the nightstand to see if there are any in there. There are none. In the drawer are several black, hard-covered books and a large manila envelope fastened with a string. It feels like it has papers in it. I pull out a couple of the books. School yearbooks. I wipe my tears with my shirt.

I flip through the pages of one. My yearbook was similar except for the hairstyles. There are no inscriptions, like mine has. I don't recognize anyone. I grab another and peruse the pages.

Finally, light is filtering through the closed drapes, but there's no noise in the other room. I grab another book and try to get comfortable.

As I'm skimming the pages, a picture catches my attention. I turn the page back and stare. It's Ma. Rather than looking at the camera directly, she's looking off to the side. Ma's hair is parted in the middle and falls straight to her shoulders.

There are pictures of Da and Paddy in their rugby uniforms. In all the pictures, they are smiling with arms linked or slung around each other and their mates.

There is a picture of the theater group. Ma's sitting on the couch with the others. Seated next to her is Mr. Walters on one side and a girl on the other. Mr. Walters's arm lies across the top of the couch directly behind Ma's head. His body is shifted toward Ma, rather than toward the arm of the couch, like he's leaning in to talk to her or get her to smile. He's wearing heavy black glasses and has hair the color of copper and a bushy mustache.

In another picture, Ma is leaning over a table while Mr. Walters appears to be talking to a group of students on the opposite end of the table. It's the group working on the school newspaper. Everyone is laughing, including Mr. Walters. Everyone but Ma.

I close the book and put it back. I'm cold, but I can't get myself under the covers, so I pull the afghan up to my chin. Not only did I not know Ma sang, I never knew she was in theater or worked on the newspaper. Her eyes seemed sad even then. Yet it looked like she had friends.

Where are those friends now?

Other questions plague me. How did she and Da, an unlikely couple, get together? Why did he have an affair?

Who did he have an affair with? How did I not see it? Why did Ma need to see Da now? Why didn't she want to see me? What am I going to do without her?

There's movement in the other room. Then Ryan peeks in.

"You're up. Grand." Ryan grabs the crutches leaning against the wall. "Let's get you something to eat and out of this room. It's a lovely day out." He is dressed in running clothes. Perspiration drips down his temples and flushed face.

He helps me to the bathroom and waits outside. It's not easy getting my pants down as I balance on the sink and hold my throbbing foot up. It takes me a long time to figure out how to do it. When I finally finish, he's there to open the door and to help me to the kitchen.

Each step takes an eternity.

Light streams in through the window above the kitchen sink, piled with dishes. The drapes in the living room are parted halfway. A pillow tops a chair next to one at the table that Ryan pulls out for me. He helps lift my foot up and offers me tea. I cringe, but mutter, "Thanks."

Mr. Walters smiles warmly. "I'll have some food for you in a minute." The table is set with china and cloth napkins. "I'm warming up the lamb from last night. Not the usual breakfast, but a specialty of mine that you won't want to miss."

When Mr. Walters places the food on the table, the aroma of lamb, garlic and onions tickles my nose. My stomach growls. I start devouring the meal. Mr. Walters and Ryan watch me while they eat scones and drink their tea. The lamb, soaked in heavy gravy, goes down easily. Some gravy drips from my mouth and I catch it with my napkin. It's rich and savory. The buttery biscuits sop up what my fork misses.

It's the first home-cooked meal I've had in a month.

Mr. Walters watches me. As I'm nearly finished, he says, "You can stay here as long as you like." He's fiddling with the button on his sweater. "It's just Johnny I've got to tend. There's plenty of room."

Touched, I smile. "Thanks, sir. But I want to go home."

"Seamus can't take care of you." Mr. Walters tosses down his napkin and folds his arms.

"He can try," I say. "Besides, I need to ask him things."

"Like what?" Mr. Walters peers over his thick glasses at me.

Ryan shoots a look that Mr. Walters doesn't catch. "Maybe that's between them, Willie."

"It's okay." I shift on the hard wooden chair. It moves slightly, scraping the floor. Taking a deep breath, I say, "I need to know about him and Ma. I found her journal right before the run. He was having an affair with some woman. Now Ma wants to see him. I need to know what will happen to them—to our family now."

Mr. Walters shakes his head and scowls. "That's ridiculous."

"It's not," I insist. "She wanted to end her life on her fortieth birthday because she couldn't live with his lies."

Mr. Walters is now leaning on the table. It wobbles on the warped, cracked linoleum. "She said that—or wrote that?"

"Not exactly, but it just makes sense now."

"What makes sense is your da would rather be at the pub than at home with his wife." Mr. Walters stomps out his cigar. "There's no other woman. Even if there was, Annie never loved him."

My lip trembles "How can you say that?"

"Because." He looks down at his stained fingernails and says softly, "I know."

Ryan scoots his chair over. He puts his arm around me. "You're shaking. Let me get you a blanket." He darts out of the room and comes back with a tightly-knit wool blanket that he wraps around my shoulders. The corner scratches my cheek.

I say, "How do you know Ma never loved Da?"

Mr. Walters pulls his glasses off, sets them near his empty plate and cup, and looks at me. He rubs the bridge of his wide nose. Then he closes his eyes and bites his thin, lower lip.

I wait.

In the distance, the bells of St. Patrick's summon people to daily mass.

Finally, Mr. Walters looks up with misty, faded blue eyes. He looks past me, not meeting my eyes. He says, "Because she loved me."

Chapter Twelve

I can feel my mouth pucker as if I'd bitten into a lemon. "It's not possible. You're so..."

"Old? Well, it's relative. Some girls prefer older men. Your mother did. We took a fancy toward each other." He peers past me into the living room, at the piano heaped with papers and sighs. "She had a voice like an angel. Really. I gave her lessons. Her parents never encouraged her so we snuck them in after school."

"I don't understand what you're saying." I pull the blanket closer.

"It started slowly, mind you. She came for lessons and gradually started opening up to me. She didn't trust other adults. Such a miserable childhood. She talked of it only to me. She'd come to my class before and then afterwards. Even joined the theater and publications group so we could be together." He looks down at his empty plate and says softly, "We didn't mean to get close. It just happened. She needed someone to listen. To be her friend."

Mr. Walters looks out the window at the grey sky.

"I don't believe you." My voice quivers. "She loved Da. Not you. She married *him*. Not you."

"That doesn't mean she didn't love me. It would have been inconvenient to marry."

"Why?"

Neither Ryan nor Mr. Walters look at me. Then Ryan says with disgust, "Because he's married."

My mouth hangs open and my eyes widen. "What? But I've never seen your wife."

Mr. Walters pushes himself up from the table. "She's gone," he says. "With our daughter." As he leans on the table, it wobbles. My cold tea splashes onto the saucer. The lines in his face deepen as he looks at me with milky, sad eyes. "You're young, but someday you might understand. We all make choices in life, but some choices are made for us. In the end, we live with them. We don't get second chances." He sighs, shakes his head and whistles for Johnny as he leaves the table and shuffles down the hall to his room.

I turn to Ryan. I'm about to uncork. "This is mad. It doesn't make any sense. Where are his wife and daughter?"

"London. My aunt, my mother's sister, left probably fifteen years ago. She just up and said they were moving. Got a job teaching music at a private school. Willie refused to go with them, even to get them settled." Ryan touches my hand, which has gone numb like the rest of my body. He says, "We don't talk much of it."

Then it hits me: What if Ma plans to come home to Mr. Walters and not to us?

I lower my leg and push back from the table. "I need to get out of here. I can't stay. I want to go home."

Ryan grabs the blanket, which has fallen to the floor, and hands me the crutches lying at my feet. "You need someone there, and I have to work tomorrow."

"I'll manage. Paddy will help until Da gets back. Fiona, even. I'm bloody well not staying here one more minute." I take a few steps, unsteady and shaking all over, while pain surges up my leg.

Ryan holds his hands up, stopping me from going anywhere. "How about we go to my flat? I have a shower stool and elevated toilet seat from when I had knee surgery a couple of years ago."

Shaking my head, I say, "I'm going home. I'm not staying with you."

"Never said you were. Paddy brought over your phone and some fresh clothes last night while you were sleeping. Let's get you changed, and we'll spend the day at my flat until your da gets back." He smiles and touches my cheek. "Humor me. I want to make sure someone is with you. And, some proper food would be in order."

If I have another choice, I don't see it.

Ryan helps me to the car and we drive toward Westport. Sitting in the car, exhausted and lost in my thoughts, I close my eyes and lean back against the seat while Ryan strums his fingers on the wheel and hums to the music.

The thought of Mr. Walters and Ma "close"—whatever that means—repulses me. I don't believe him. Did I miss something? I try to think back to times that I saw Ma talk to him or even mention him, but I can't. I can barely imagine Ma intimate with Da. And certainly not with "Weird Willie," as Fiona referred to him. I shudder and try to think of anything else, but I can't. Even my burning ankle doesn't distract me long.

What else am I missing?

When we arrive at Ryan's flat, he helps me out, waiting patiently as I stump to the door. Inside, sun streams in from large windows overlooking the quiet residential street. He ushers me to a leather couch facing the largest flat screen television I've ever seen. It's mounted above a gas fireplace on a wall the color of yellow daffodils. A guitar is propped on a stand in the corner near a desk with pictures that I can't see from the couch.

After offering me a glass of water and my pills, he grabs an assortment of brightly-colored pillows from the side chairs and elevates my leg, then stuffs one pillow under my head. He sits on the oversized ottoman facing me. I glide my hand over the soft leather. "Nice. You live here long?"

"Not really. I moved in when I started working with my dad. I couldn't stand the idea of living at home after being on my own so many years. For an only child it can be suffocating."

"Tell me about it."

"They thought I'd never come back after university and my travels, so they make it easy for me to stay around."

"I'm leaving Louisburgh as soon as Ma is better. It's so provincial here. There's got to be more," I say. "Something better."

"There's more. Some better. Some not." He rests his hand on my mine. I notice small lines around his eyes and wonder what he's seen outside of Westport. Outside of Ireland.

"I'm going to run to the store quick," Ryan says. He hands me my phone, the remote, and a few magazines that were scattered on the ottoman: the Economist, Veterinary Journal, Architectural Digest, and Runner's World. "You okay with these and the telly?"

"Grand."

He gets up and covers me with a furry wool blanket and then leaves. I sink into the soft, chocolate-colored couch and pull the blanket close. It smells like a bouquet of spring flowers, not like ours that reek of peat. I pick up Runner's World. The mailing label has Ryan's address but another name: Alex Murphy. I start reading but soon fall asleep.

~

The door slams, and I wake up with a jolt. For a moment I don't know where I am. Then I remember. I lift my head, expecting Ryan. Instead, walking through the door, carrying bags of groceries, is a tall, blonde woman wearing Ray-Ban sunglasses.

"Hi." The woman glides into the room, sets the groceries on the table, and flips her sunglasses up onto her head. "I'm Alex."

"Oh, I'm Eliza." I pull myself up from my slouch. "Ryan's gone for food."

She feigns exasperation. "Go figure. We'll have enough for a party." With a face like a model, she laughs and tosses up her perfectly manicured hands. "He eats like a bull but burns it like a jaguar. Always on the move, that bloke."

My smile feels forced, but I hope she doesn't notice. Her face looks familiar, like someone I might have seen in a magazine or on a commercial. I catch myself staring and say, "I'm just here because he's helping me on account…"

"Oh, of course. You're the girl. How sad. Yes, he told me he was helping you get back on your feet—so to speak." She flips her mane back and laughs. I bristle at "girl." Then with a syrupy tone, she asks, "What can I do to make you comfortable? Want juice? A Coke? Oh, never mind. We haven't any. Ryan thinks it's dreadfully bad for the body. More water?"

"Water's lovely. I'll be gone soon." I assure her. "He's just loaning me things. For when I'm on my own."

"I'll be back in a jiff." In her skinny jeans, she prances to the kitchen, smiling. Her teeth are the whitest I've ever seen. I run my tongue over my teeth, which feel scummy.

I try not to stare at Alex but I can't stop myself. She's so perfect. I tuck my dirty hair behind my ear and, when Alex isn't looking, I wet my fingers and try to smooth my thick, disheveled hair. I smell stale. Pinching my cheeks, I try adding color to my pale skin.

Just then, Ryan bounds through the door with an armful of groceries. Spying Alex near the fridge, he sets the groceries down, pecks her on the cheek, and says, "Hello, beautiful."

I just barely survive the rest of the afternoon and our meal together. I listen to Ryan and Alex banter back and forth. Finally I insist that I must go home. My foot, I say, is killing me. And it is. During the drive back, Ryan lectures me about caring for my ankle. I mutter grateful responses, counting the minutes until I can be alone.

For a moment, snuggling into Ryan's couch, I had pictured what a relationship with a real man might be. Not like with Mikey or others before him, who wanted only one thing, and who moved on once they got it. Or maybe I was the one who moved on. I never wanted a serious relationship. Especially with Mikey. I always wanted more. Better. I just didn't know what—or who—"better" was.

I thought I saw better in Ryan.

Chapter Thirteen

Smoke drifts from the chimney of our cottage. Da's car is there, as is one that I don't recognize. When I finally make it up the path and into the cottage, Fiona bursts towards me. "Eliza, darling. I came over when I got your text." She tries to hug me, but Ryan blocks her so I don't teeter and fall back.

"Thanks for coming," I say. "I don't know what I'd do without you." It surprises me that emotion catches in my throat.

"You'll never know, love."

Standing near the fireplace with their hands in their pockets are two men I don't recognize. They smile awkwardly.

Fiona squeals, "You must meet my two favorite Americans. Remember I told you about them? We went to Galway together. See? You should have come with us. This would never have happened." She pushes past Ryan, who is trying to get pillows arranged under my aching foot, and links her arm through the slightly–built American with slicked-back hair. "This is Jake," she says, making his name sound like a snack she's about to bite into. Fiona flutters her eyes at him. Then she pulls the other man over. "And this is Jake's friend Hunter." Hunter, muscular and tall, has short-cropped hair the color of fertile soil and stubble covering his square jaw. Rugged and handsome, he nods an acknowledgment.

Fiona watches Ryan as he adjusts my pillows, puts my medicine on the table, and brings me a water bottle. "Aren't you a good doctor," she says.

"Least I could do." Ryan hands Fiona the discharge documents. "Make sure she follows up, especially if she has any of these symptoms." He rattles them off and points to something on the papers. Fiona squints her eyes. I know she's only pretending to be interested.

Ryan tells me to call and text—to keep him up to date on how things are going or if he can help—and I agree. Leaning down, he kisses my cheek. I want him to stay as much as I want him to go. Then I picture him and Alex curled on the couch watching the television in front of the fake fire. My stomach tightens.

After Ryan gently closes the door, Fiona mocks Ryan's instructions: "Remember, no alcohol while on the meds." Jake bursts out laughing. This only encourages Fiona. Hunter folds his arms across his broad chest and rolls his eyes.

I shift on the couch, my ankle throbbing. "Where's Da?"

"Passed out on his bed," Fiona says.

"Right."

"As your best friend, I'm getting you out. You need some craic."

"Did you not hear Ryan? I have to keep my leg propped. I can't drink," I remind her.

"Well, I can drink, and so can Jake and Hunter. You can prop your bum leg up just as easily at Paddy's. We can get you set up in the corner. We'll take the pillows with us. There are three of us who can help you."

"I feel like shite. I just want to be home. With you. *Only you.*"

"But I told Jake and Hunter we'd go out." Fiona pouts her

painted lips. She says, "There's nothing to do here. The time for fun is now. If you wait for it, you might miss it." Fiona's tone suggests this is a deep thought.

Jake snickers. "Yeah, baby. That's right. Life's short." His dark, beady eyes and hooked nose make him look like a weasel.

Hunter steps forward and slaps Jake's shoulder. "Let's blow. They need time, and I'm wiped from all the driving we've done in the past few days. You'll be fine without her one night. Remember what life was like before you became a hapless fool."

Jake whines, "But I want to be with Fiona." Pathetic. Fiona puckers her lips, and he leans down to kiss her.

I start crying. It's the last thing I want to do. Fiona comes over, wraps her arm around me and purrs, "Oh, darling. Don't. It's alright. I'm here for you, love."

Shrugging her arm off my shoulders, I say, "Go. Leave me alone. I'm fine without you."

Stunned, Fiona glares at me like I slapped her. I look away. She gets up in a huff and mouths to Jake, "I tried." Jake escorts her out like she's Mother Teresa. Hunter says good-bye and saunters out behind them.

The cold air sweeps in, sending shivers down my spine. Then the door slams, and I'm alone. Staring at the smoldering embers and the darkening sky, I listen for Da's snores. Faint. Steady. Familiar. I reach for the crutches, propped against the arm of the couch, and hoist myself up. Each painful step brings me closer to my room.

Sleep eludes me. I toss and turn all night and rise early in the morning. Da emerges from his room in wrinkled trousers and a half-tucked shirt. His face bears pillow marks. At first he doesn't see me as he tromps to the refrigerator, opens it wide, and stares into it. It's empty except for green bread and brown lettuce. I know because I looked there earlier for something to eat.

He looks in the cupboard. "God dammit," he says with his back still to me.

"Time to make a proper trip to the store, or we'll starve to death." I have thought all night about what to say to him. This wasn't it.

He turns, sees my elevated leg and grimaces. "Holy Mother Mary, what the hell happened to you?"

"I broke my ankle running Croagh Patrick and had to have surgery. Didn't Paddy tell you?"

"Haven't talked to him." Shaking his head, he walks over and looks at my leg more closely. "It's not smart to run up that damn mountain alone."

"I wasn't alone. Doc's son was running with me and he helped me down."

"Thank the saints." Da runs his hands through his disheveled hair and sits down in the chair opposite me. "What are you going to do now? How will you work at the B&B?"

"Don't mind me. I'll figure it out." I push myself up. The blanket slips off, to the floor, and I shiver. The fire had long gone out, and I didn't make it over to toss on more peat. I reach for the blanket, not quite out of reach, and pull it up over my shoulders. Da doesn't move to help me.

I say, "How's Ma?" Da, rubbing his greying beard, looks at me with tired eyes.

I sit forward, causing the blanket to fall from my shoulders. "Is she coming home?"

He avoids my eyes. "Might never, she says."

"What?" A chill climbs my spine. "Wait. Why did she want to see *you*?"

Da shakes his head and avoids my eyes. "That's between us."

"I want to know."

"Some things are between a man and his wife," he says as he twirls his wedding ring. "It didn't pertain to you. But she asked how you were getting by, and I told her you were just fine, but not many guests this season. Not yet, anyway."

"You could at least tell me what the hell is going on."

His voice booms. "Shite, I don't bloody know. For Christ's sake, she won't tell *me* why she did it." He melts into the chair. "She doesn't know if she can come back." Sighing, he says in a voice, barely loud enough for me to hear, "Tell me, where the hell will she go?"

"You did this to her." My tone is icy.

He glares at me. "What the hell? How is this *my* fault?"

"You drove her away with your affair with some slut. That's why she took off her ring—not that you noticed." It's still on my hand. I wave it at him. "So, *who* is she?"

"Jaysus! You're off your nut. Where the hell did you get that idea?"

"It makes sense," I say.

"Nothing makes sense. You're mental. They give you something at the hospital to send you off your rocker?"

"Paddy said you had to marry her because of me." I narrow my eyes in contempt. "You never loved her, did you?"

"Christ. I got to go." He grabs his jacket and slams the door shut on his way out. I know where he's heading: To Paddy's. Though I have no idea when he'll come home—or in what state.

Chapter Fourteen

Maeve Cunningham arrives, the last person I had wanted to call. She's bent over from the weight of an overstuffed bag slung over her arm, two bags of groceries, and the wind pounding her face as she walks from her car. I've been watching for her from a chair near the door. She said she was on her way. The last thing I want to do is make her wait. Not a good start.

Leaning on the crutches, I swing the door open so she can get by. The wind gusts in, and the cold air slaps my face.

"Never mind the door. I'll get it. Just sit your arse down before you catch cold as well." Maeve sets the groceries on the table. One bag falls over. From it spills fresh fruit, vegetables, butter, eggs, and meat.

Whipping her coat off, Maeve struts back to the door, shuts it, and then flings her coat over the back of the faded couch. She thrusts peat turves into the fireplace, lights them and replaces the screen. On her way back to the kitchen, she squats, picks up my blanket, which had slipped from my shoulders to the floor, and places it over the back of the couch.

Maeve's sweater, the color of mud, stretches over her wide hips and the tummy tire left from giving birth to the twin babies. Scanning the cottage, she sighs, and her mouth twitches disapprovingly. Dishes fill the sink and remnants of food dust the counters and table. There is an odor of moldy bread lingering. She runs a hand through her short, mousy hair. Standing there with her feet apart and arms crossed over her full bosom, she says, "Aren't you supposed to have that leg up?"

"Oh, yeah," I mumble back at her. I hobble to the table, pulling out one chair to sit on and another on which to prop my foot.

"Oh, for Christ's sake, you need it higher than that." Maeve huffs over to the couch and grabs a pillow. She lifts my leg and puts it on the pillow. Then she turns away.

"Thanks," I mutter.

Maeve rolls her eyes. "You asked. I came." She turns to the refrigerator and starts putting things away. "Pretty stupid thing from what I hear. You're lucky Doc's son was there."

"I suppose."

My swallowed pride sits in my throat like the horse pills I have been taking. In the weeks since Ma's...accident, I have talked only briefly to Maeve. When I've had to.

We'd passed each other on the street not too long after the day I found Ma in the tub. She'd said she was sorry to hear about Ma and asked if there was anything she could do. I knew she always was looking for more hours with her husband, Bobby, not working. I told her there weren't any guests coming for nearly a month. I told her that I had it handled—and until I broke my ankle, I did.

Now I need her. I can't work. Granda would expect to know I had this managed until he got back. Since Maeve was coming over to get the key, I'd asked if she'd mind picking up some groceries. I said I'd pay her back.

Maeve moves with purpose. She puts things away, fills the sink with hot, soapy water, and begins wiping down the counters, the cabinet handles, and the table where I'm sitting. She doesn't look at me. I smell her familiar body odor. Sweat beads on her wide, shiny forehead.

"You don't need to do that. I just needed some food," I say. "Da's useless."

"You just figure that out?" She arranges the salt and pepper shakers in the center of the table. She mumbles, "They all are."

I don't want to, but I ask, "So, how's your brother?"

She snorts. "Mikey's useless, too. You know that."

Maeve opens the cabinets, grabs a pen and a crumpled piece of paper from her purse, scribbles something, and then stuffs the paper back into her purse.

Six years older than Mikey and me, Maeve doesn't look at all like her brother. She's as stout as he's tall. Her dark eyes don't twinkle when she talks to you. They glare at you with judgment and expectation. The last time she wore smart clothes was just before she found out she was having her babies. I can't remember Maeve ever laughing or going to the pub. Except to haul Bobby home.

Granda describes Maeve as "dependable." She is that.

I shift on the hard, wooden chair. "Thanks for covering for me at the B&B. Obviously I can't for awhile. Until I move better. There are guests scheduled next week."

She's back rummaging and not looking at me. "I'll manage it." Grabbing a bowl, she cracks four eggs and whisks them with milk and slides them into the buttered skillet. I don't tell her that I prefer eggs fried.

There's a lot I don't tell Maeve.

Maeve heaps the eggs on a plate and sets it down in front

of me. "Better get some meat on those bones." She plops down on a chair and waits, watching me. Famished, I dig in.

As I eat, we discuss the logistics of tending the B&B. This is the most we've ever talked or spent time together. Later, while Maeve is cleaning up, I send Granda an email explaining everything to him, including the fact that Maeve has the key and will manage things until I'm better. I still will track reservations. I can do that with my laptop. Maeve will check phone messages when she stops by the B&B.

Just when I think Maeve is ready to leave, she rolls up the sleeves of her frayed sweater and marches down the hall to the bathroom. She returns with towels and shampoo.

"What are you doing?"

"You need a wash." She lifts my leg down and pushes the chair in. "Lean over the sink and I'll help you." She starts running the water.

I protest. Maeve glares at me and says, "You look like shite."

"Really, I can manage."

Maeve snorts. "I don't have all day, so get your sorry arse over here."

I see from her set expression that there's no arguing with her. I make it to the sink, support my weight on my good leg, and bend my head down. Maeve drenches my thick hair with tepid water and lathers it. It smells like lilacs. Her stumpy fingers massage my scalp. My eyes close. Water drips down my neck. I shudder. Maeve catches it with the towel. After she's applied the conditioner and rinsed it away, she wraps my head in the fluffy towel and tells me to wait for a minute before walking, in case I'm dizzy from leaning over.

I tell her I'm fine. She shakes her head and hands me my

crutches. "Then start heading to your room," she commands, every bit a Garda drill sergeant. I don't argue.

With each small step, she's behind me, and when I finally reach my bed, she flips back the covers, helps me onto the bed, and arranges the pillows. She sets my laptop on the nightstand. It's within reach, along with a glass of water and my medicine. The curtains remain open to the grey day while the awkward silence hangs between us.

When Maeve turns to leave, I thank her. A small smile tweaks her mouth, but only for a moment. She mutters as she walks out the door, "It's what your granda would want me to do."

~

The day is long, but my patience is not.

Having managed a satisfactory night's sleep, I sit propped in bed, checking our reservations at the B&B. There are several new inquiries. I confirm dates and logistics. Later, Granda replies to my email, tells me how unfortunate my situation is, and promises to call when he has better cell phone reception. He doesn't ask about Ma.

I stare out the window, waiting for something. What? I don't know. But it's all the same. It's just a different day. The same grey sky. The same rain. The same wind. Even when I'm able to move better, and even run again, it will be the same. I'll go out with Fiona for craic. We won't talk about what happened. We'll toss the pints back and laugh. We'll talk about everyone's business. We'll tell the tourists there's no finer place in Ireland and that they're family now. But nothing is what it appears. No one is who they seem to be.

I've gone to the bathroom several times and even made myself a sandwich. I can't believe how exhausted I am from doing nothing all day.

I reach over and turn on the lamp on the end table where I've set my laptop. I consider reading, but don't have any books or magazines handy, and I don't have the energy to get up.

Without anything to do, I let images flood my memory. The one that always comes is Ma's eyes looking at me in the tub and her ashen skin in the ambulance. I think of all the things I would tell her if she would see me. I consider writing her a letter, but none of the words come out right. Even if Da was having an affair, why not just leave him? I could have gone with her. We could have moved to Galway. I have money saved, and Granda could loan us more. What I don't understand is how she could have left me here alone with Da. In Louisburgh. Did she expect me to take care of Da now?

The door slams, jolting me back. There are voices: Paddy and Da.

Paddy hollers, "Hallo, sweetheart." His shoes tap down the hall. He raps on the door, opens it and smiles. His jet black hair shows no sign of grey, unlike Da's. "There you are. Had to see you for myself. Jaysus, you're quite the sight. I didn't know it was this bad. Saints be praised, it wasn't worse."

Da clomps down the hall to the bathroom in his wading boots and slams the door. He doesn't stop in to check on me.

Paddy sits on the edge of the bed in his pressed trousers and starched shirt. He asks me all about how it happened and groans when I tell him about the bone snapping and getting down the mountain, the long wait in the emergency room, and surgery.

Just like when I was a child and talked to him about the

mean girls, Paddy strokes my hair and says, "You poor thing. It's all going to be fine now, don't you worry." He pulls me close and his wool jacket tickles my face. He smells like peat. Like his pub. Like home.

I let him hold me. After awhile I say, "Paddy, there are things that confuse me. What I mean is, I'm wondering about Ma."

Paddy groans. "We've had this talk."

"No, it's something else. I want to know about Mr. Walters and Ma. He was her teacher, right?"

Paddy's face relaxes. "Sure. He taught music. All of us had him at one time or another."

"Right. Mr. Walters said he and Ma were close."

Paddy laughs. "Willie fancies himself close to all the lasses. He wasn't as patient with the lads. But, hell, I never noticed him pay much attention to your ma. She stuck to herself. Even back then." He pauses and then says, "Except for Linda."

"What about Linda," Da bellows as he walks into the room.

Paddy turns. "Remember how Annie stuck like glue to Linda in school?"

Da, with his hair sticking up and wearing his waders and fishing jacket, stinks like fish. "Hell, I haven't thought about her in years."

I raise myself up. "I saw a yearbook. Ma was in choir and publications. Mr. Walters supervised both."

Paddy shrugs. "Don't recall if your ma was involved or not. Linda headed both up. So it makes sense your ma tagged along."

I say, "He said Ma and he were close. What does that mean?"

Da laughs, "It means shite. Willie always fancied himself

a charmer. Remember, Paddy, how he was sugar-sweet with Linda? His star student."

Paddy nods. "It bothered him when Linda went to school in London. Fit to be tied. Hell if I know why." Paddy turns to me. "Linda made us promise to take Annie under our wing. She didn't have any friends except Linda."

"Me, not you." Da slaps Paddy on the back. "She fancied you an eejit."

"She's the only woman who could refuse my charm." Paddy's eyes look tired and sad. "Nothing I did pleased her."

Da fiddles with the zipper on his jacket and says, "Forget about it."

I look back and forth at Da and Paddy. "What am I missing?"

"Nothing." Paddy exchanges a look with Da. They both avoid my eyes.

"I want to know." I'm aware that I'm raising my voice and I don't care. I look at Da who hoists himself up and walks to the window.

I wait. The only sound is the wind rattling the panes.

"Tell me," I say.

Da finally turns towards me and says, "I dunno. It seemed your ma didn't fancy *any* man much."

"What are you saying?" I squeak.

Paddy casts Da a look to shut up, but Da misses it. He says, "Your ma fancied lasses. Or at least Linda."

"That can't be." The air is sucked out of my chest.

"'Tis true. I didn't know until I married her." Da tosses his arms up in the air.

Paddy turns to me. "I thought your ma just hated me. Because of Linda liking me and all."

"Made your ma mad as a hornet that Linda liked Paddy."

Nothing makes sense. I shift, sending a bolt of pain up my leg. When the pain subsides, I say, "But you and Ma. I don't get it."

Da runs his hands through his disheveled hair and shakes his head. "I'm going out." Then he clomps out of the room in his boots.

Paddy looks like he's going to say something, but he closes his mouth and follows Da.

Chapter Fifteen

I scoot to the edge of the bed and grab the crutches. My hands, raw and blistered, grip the pads. With burning palms, I hoist myself up and call for them to wait. There's no response. Their voices rise and fall, but I can't make out the words. Pain sears through my ankle and shoots up my leg as I thump out of my room and down the hall.

When I finally get to the main room, Da's yanking his coat on, and Paddy's blocking him from leaving. The outside light above the door casts a dim glow in the room. Paddy's face is twisted in a scowl, and his voice is so low that I can't hear what he's saying. Da's brushing off Paddy's hands.

"Tell me. I need to know." I stop in the shadows of the doorway and try to catch my breath. "Why did she marry you?"

Da almost falls backwards when Paddy releases his arm, but he catches his balance and leans back against the door frame, turning but not looking at me.

I limp forward, out of the shadows. "What the hell aren't you telling me?" I demand. "Ma's in a mental hospital and she'll see you but not me. But you won't help me understand a feckin' thing."

"There's nothing." Da has a bottle of whiskey in his hand that he tries to hide inside his fishing jacket.

I glare at him through hair that has fallen over my face. I can't brush the strand of hair aside without losing my balance. I say, "I'm not a child anymore."

"You're *her* child," Da whispers. "It's not my place to tell."

"Tell what? And whaddya mean, 'her' child?"

Paddy comes over. "Love, you should sit down." He places his hand on the low of my back and guides me to the couch. Grabbing a pillow, he lifts my ankle onto it.

Paddy hollers at Da to sit down. Da sulks over and falls in the chair but looks down at his boots. The whiskey bottle peeks out from the large inside pocket of his jacket. He pulls the jacket closed.

As I try to adjust my leg to relieve the burning and throbbing, Paddy tosses peat into the fireplace. The fire starts to warm the air but not the space between Da and me.

Eyes narrowed, I hiss, "*You* did this to her."

Da's ruddy face falls. He looks out the dark window. The open curtains reveal the night sky. The wind, straight off Clew Bay, whistles through the cracks. Neither Da nor Paddy says anything. I'm about to break the silence when Paddy, who is standing by Da's chair, tosses up his hands. "Your da's a bloody saint, he is. He's no more responsible for what your ma did than the man in the moon."

"Shut up, Paddy," Da snarls.

"Your ma got herself pregnant by who-knows-who, and your da married her. Just like that. He found her bloody, half-naked body in the pasture…"

"Enough, Paddy!" Da pounds his hand on the coffee table, sending the magazines to the floor and causing me to jump.

"She has a right to know," Paddy bellows.

"No." Squinting and leaning forward with his hands on

the arms of the chair, Da looks ready to charge Paddy.

I say, "You found her *naked* in a pasture?"

Paddy turns to me. "We don't know what happened. We saw her the night before. Hell, Linda *made* us invite her out since she had no other friends."

Da bellows, "Jaysus, can't you shut your bloody mouth?"

Paddy ignores Da. "Annie wasn't used to drinking and she lost it on the street. Then she decided to walk home. It wasn't far. This is when they lived down the street here—at the B&B—not at the new house where your grandparents live now." He looks at Da, who is staring at the peat fire. "She wouldn't let us walk her home. We tried."

My heart races. "What?"

Da's bushy brows furrow as he rubs the stubble of his weathered face. "The next morning, I was walking toward town. Something caught my eye in the pasture." He licks his lips and says softly, "It looked like a sick animal, but the sun was just rising so I couldn't see so good. I went closer to get a better look, and I saw it was a person. At first I thought it was some bloke who got plastered and fell asleep on his way home." Da looks out the window at the darkness and says, "She didn't have any pants on and she was shivering and bleeding."

I clasp my hands on my mouth. "Oh, my God!"

Paddy says, "Your da found her clothes scattered in the field, helped her dress, and took her in. A real saint."

"Shut the hell up, Paddy." Da shifts in the chair, pushing the bottle deeper under his jacket.

Paddy touches my shaking shoulder. I pull back. "Who'd you call for help? The Garda? Granda? Linda?" Everything is whirling in my head. A dream. A nightmare. Not my life. Not Ma's.

"Hell, I couldn't understand half her blathering." Da throws his hands up. "She wouldn't let me call anyone. I tried to take her home, but she started going crazy. I just took her back to my place. No one was home because everyone went to visit my brother in Glasgow for the weekend."

"But who? I mean, did she know who..."

Da shakes his head. "No. She was drunk. Didn't remember anything. She was scared that she might get pregnant and have to tell her parents."

"I don't understand how you..."

"Married her? Hell, Eliza, when it turned out she was pregnant, what could I do?"

"See, your da's a bloody saint!"

"Shut your gob, Paddy." The lines around his eyes soften. "Before she found out she was pregnant, I guess she didn't want to be alone and didn't have anyone to talk to about... well, what happened...and we got close. Once."

"*Close*? But, I thought you said she didn't like men."

"She did then." A heavy sigh escapes Da's downturned mouth. "When she told me that she was pregnant, it seemed right to marry her."

"I don't believe this."

Da leans toward me. His disheveled hair flops into his lined face, which is close enough that I can smell the whiskey on his breath. "It was the right thing to do. I couldn't leave her pregnant and all." His eyes mist. "Besides, I got you."

Da reaches out to touch my hand, but I yank it back and say, "You're not even my father?"

His chest heaves and tears fall as he collapses his head into his chafed hands. "I dunno. You've always been my Eliza baby." I've never seen Da cry. At least not when he's sober.

Paddy says, "'Tis true." He tries to pat my shoulder, but I jerk it away.

My gut feels like someone kicked me.

There's a single knock and the door swings open. Fiona bursts through with Jake and Hunter, her new best friends—the Americans on holiday—trailing. "Hello, darling. We've brought the fun to you since you can't go out with that gammy leg." She flips her hair back, thrusts her chest out, and holds up a bottle of Jameson. As she struts to the couch, she winks at Jake and motions for him to follow, which he does. Hunter hangs back with a bag of crisps tucked under his arm.

Da wipes his eyes and hoists himself up. "I'll not get in your way." He pulls out his own bottle of whiskey, holds it up, and says as he walks out the door, "To your fun."

Chapter Sixteen

Cold barges in with a gale force as Da leaves with Paddy. Shuddering, I lift my leg down and make room for Fiona on the couch. She plops next to me and sets the bottle of Jameson in the center of the coffee table. No doubt she took it from Paddy's while he was here with Da. She flashes Hunter a wide smile. "Oh, bloody hell, I forgot the glasses. Be a love, Hunter, and get them from the kitchen." Hunter goes searching for glasses. Jake sidles up next to Fiona, who is sandwiched between us. I shift closer to the arm of the couch.

As Hunter returns with the glasses, Fiona prattles on about how testy Maeve was the other day when she saw her at the chemist. "A real pain in me hole," Fiona says. Jake kisses her rosy cheek and she giggles. Hunter looks bored. His eyes land on the pictures on the fireplace mantel. There's one of Fiona and me in our princess outfits and another one taken on the last day of school. As long as I can remember, we dreamed of the places, imagined and real, that we'd go.

At some point we stopped talking of going away. We stopped talking about our dreams.

Fiona hands me a full glass of whiskey, which I take. It burns my nose and turns my stomach. I set it down. Jake offers Fiona a cigarette and lights it for her. Sucking it with her brightly painted lips, she inhales, closes her shimmering eyes and then exhales. Jake tries catching the lofting smoke into his mouth. Fiona lets out a high-pitched squeal.

After locking lips with Jake, Fiona untangles herself. "Oh my God. Darling, I almost forgot to tell you. The most dreadful thing happened." Fiona sweeps her short fringe aside and drains her glass. Jake refills it, nearly to the top. "We went to Galway the other day. You know the store we love? The one with the great shoes. Get this…" Fiona pauses and waits for everyone to look at her. Then, with dramatic flair, she says, "The damn store has closed and now it's a *Starbucks*."

Fiona tosses her hands up, forgetting she's holding the glass. "Oh, shite. Look what I've done."

"I'm looking, baby." Jake's hand grazes Fiona's shirt. "And I like what I see."

They melt into each other laughing. Hunter gets up, goes to the kitchen, and returns with a hand towel. "Here," he says, tossing the towel at Fiona, who makes no attempt to catch it. Instead, she reaches for the bottle of Jameson.

I lurch forward and snatch the bottle before she does.

Fiona stares at me, her heavily-lined almond eyes wide. "Do you want more, too?"

"I do want more," I growl.

"Then take some and pass it here," says Fiona, challenging me.

Mute and breathing shallow, I clutch the bottle.

Fiona pouts. She reaches for the bottle. I bury it further under my arm. Squinting her eyes, she says, "What the hell's wrong with you?"

My heart beats fast. I feel weighed down, as if sand gathered from the beaches along Clew Bay was bagged and heaped on my chest, crushing my breath. I can't escape. My insides feel like a pressure cooker, churning and boiling. Ready to erupt. I fling the bottle. It crashes at Fiona's feet. Shards of glass skitter to the corners of the room and amber fluid splashes all over the warped, wooden floor.

Fiona screeches, "Holy, shite. You've gone mental. What the—"

Glaring at Fiona, I shout, "Get out!" No one moves. Scooting to the edge of the couch, I grab my crutches. "*Now.*" Swiping at the bits of glass with the rubber tip of my crutches, I get my bearing and stand. Everyone stares at me, but no one says anything. Glass is scattered everywhere. No one offers to clean it up. No one offers to help me.

Instead, Fiona shrinks into the couch like a dog that's been kicked. Jake wraps his spindly arms around her. I wait, thinking Fiona will know what to do, but she turns away and buries her head in Jake's shoulder.

I've never yelled at Fiona. Not even when we were children and she cut the hair off all my dolls. Not even when she took my car without asking and left it at the side of the road outside a pub in Westport when she got a lift home from someone else. Not even when I found out the person she left with—and then slept with—was Mikey. Even with all that, Fiona was the one who helped me to escape the silence of my home.

A sour taste rises from deep inside and settles in my mouth. Gripping the pads on the crutches, I thump down the hall to my room. Even as I make my way down the narrow, dark hall, I think Fiona might come after me and ask what's wrong.

I collapse onto my bed and smash the pillow over my

face, overtaken by sobs. I want to scream, for them to go away and leave me alone. Yet I hold out hope that Fiona will unlock from the stranger's arms and come into my room. I wait to feel her arm soft on my heaving back.

Finally, I lift my head and listen carefully. The wind has died down. There are low voices, but no words I can make out. Then there are footsteps crunching broken glass, and the door slams shut.

I'm alone again. A stranger in a place that once felt like home.

Chapter Seventeen

My bedroom is dark when Da comes home. First I hear him shuffle down the hall and stop at my closed door. One light knock. Then the door creaks open. Soft footsteps come toward me. I smell the cigar smoke on his jacket and whiskey on his breath as he leans over the bed. My eyes remain shut, my body still. It feels like forever that he's standing there. Finally he turns, walks away, and closes my door. His scent lingers for a while, then evaporates.

When I wake up, Da is gone. Hobbling out of my room, I look down the narrow hall and notice Da's bedroom door is open and his bed, normally unmade, is stripped. When I get to the main room, I expect to clean up the broken glass and Jameson, but it's already done. Da's jacket is gone along with his tackle box.

On the kitchen table is a scone from the bakery. My favorite. Next to it, scribbled on a piece of paper, Da wrote, "I'm sorry."

I toss the paper and eat the scone.

Two months pass. The only person I've talked to is Maeve. Sometimes Granda checks in, but then he calls Maeve for the full update. Mostly, I stay inside, trying to build strength in my ankle and avoid Da. Fiona and I text, but have nothing to say. Nothing is the same.

Today, after weeks of grey skies and relentless rain, the sun shines bright. A warm breeze brushes my cheek as I stand outside the cottage, leaning on my crutches. The sunlight stings my eyes, which have grown accustomed to the dark cottage. I close my eyes and inhale deeply the sweet air. Warmth floods my face. I imagine my ankle strong and my legs carrying me over the beaten path overlooking Clew Bay and the Bunowen River, over each embedded rock and around each bend. I feel each breath rising from deep in my chest and escaping through my open mouth.

"Hey there." A voice I don't recognize startles me, and I almost topple over.

Opening my eyes, I see Hunter. He's not wearing a jacket, just a faded t-shirt, jeans and hiking boots.

I muster a smile, and he strides over. His hair, cropped short when I first met him months ago, is longer now and the stubble that had shadowed his face is a well-trimmed beard.

He leans against my car and points at my leg. "Moving better?"

I stand up straighter to demonstrate that I don't have to lean on the crutches for support. "Almost good as new."

"I'll be damned." His eyes, the color of shadowed hillsides, are either laughing at me or pleased at the progress. I can't tell.

We chat about how nice the weather finally is. He agrees

that there's no finer place than Ireland in the spring. He tells me that's why he extended his time here. I don't ask about Fiona, and he doesn't volunteer anything.

I hear squeaking and, from the corner of my eye, I see Mr. Walters pedaling his three-wheeled bicycle down the road with Johnny perched in the wire basket on the back. A cigar dangles from his mouth. Despite the warm May day, he's wearing a wool coat and tweed hat. He doesn't turn or look in my direction.

Hunter asks if I want to walk down to the beach.

I grimace. "That might be interesting. It'll take forever. What with the crutches."

"I'm not in any hurry," he says.

"You may be sorry you said that," I tell him. My calloused hands grip the handles of the crutches and I start down the uneven road. Hunter's boots crunch on the gravel.

Soon the road ends and a narrow path to the sandy beach begins. Large rocks border the beach. Hunter offers his arm and I lean on him as I lower myself to sit on one of the larger rocks. Wiping my brow, I look out at the calm water under the cloudless sky. Hunter sits beside me. With his well-shaped sideburns accentuating his high cheekbones, he looks like someone you'd see in a truck commercial.

"That's the most activity I've seen since I got here." Hunter points at the kayakers alongside the swimmers hugging the rugged shoreline. Another group of people watch from shore.

"They're training for the triathlon coming up." My gut feels hollow recalling my own unused wetsuit hanging in the closet. I squint and look for Ryan. Would he be part of this group or training on his own?

Hunter's square jaw juts forward, and he shakes his head. "Seems stupid."

"What?"

"A triathlon. Why put yourself through that?"

"It's something to do." My breath is still rapid and my leg throbs from the walk. "To push yourself."

"Plenty of ways to push yourself other than swimming in frigid water that you could drown in."

"That's the challenge," I say.

"I'd rather feel the ground under my feet." He leans back on his muscular arms and stares at the cadre of people in the water.

The soft breeze off the water carries the blended scent of fish and blooming vegetation. Boats angle in the distance. I turn to Hunter, who is staring straight ahead like he's trying to count the hundreds of small islands speckling Clew Bay, and say, "Where are you from again?"

"Montana." His voice is low and deep.

"Never known anyone from there, Do you miss it?"

Hunter reaches down and pulls out a clump of grass and turns it over in his hands until the dirt falls off. "Some parts I miss." He tosses the grass aside. "Other parts I don't."

He shifts and now his leg touches mine. He doesn't seem to notice. I don't move.

Several swimmers emerge from the water and begin unzipping their wetsuits. Propped against the rock wall close to the water are bicycles. The second leg. Today they are doing bricks, the back-to-back training to build stamina for the race. It was in the training program Ryan sent to me. I watch them transition from the water to the bicycles. Some wobble, trying to get their land legs. A few topple over trying to get out of their rubber armor. Hoots of encouragement and laughter rise from the support crew. I don't recognize anyone.

"You miss *that*?" Hunter's voice rings with either sarcasm or disbelief.

I nod. "It was going to me my first triathlon. It just would've been nice to see if I could do it."

"I guess." Hunter's voice lingers on the breeze.

I recognize Ryan running toward us along the path. He's gripping the handlebars as he runs alongside his bike. He's getting ready to mount at the road. Shorts cover his lean thighs like a second skin. He focuses straight ahead, eyes narrowed with intensity beneath the visor of his racing helmet.

I sink back on the rock, trying to merge with Hunter's shadow. Looking away, I imagine myself invisible, like a child playing peek-a-boo. I hold my breath.

He's nearly past when he stops and turns to look at me. Breathlessly, he says, "Eliza?"

My breath escapes as I sit forward. Forcing a smile, I try to stifle the thumping in my chest. "Hallo, Ryan."

His face contorts as he says, "You never returned my calls or emails."

A tight band constricts in my chest. I look down, avoiding his penetrating eyes. "Yeah, well...Sorry. I've been busy."

Ryan looks straight at Hunter. He looks like he might say something when one of his friends shouts at him to hurry up. He grips his bike and mutters, "Right." Then he quickens his pace to catch up with his mates .

Many days I started to call him or respond to his emails or text messages, but then I'd wonder what he and Alex were doing at that moment. Enjoying a nice meal together? Snuggling on the couch watching a movie and sipping a French wine? I wondered why in the hell he'd bother calling. Except maybe he still felt guilty about the fall and break.

When I can't see Ryan any longer, I hoist myself up, turn to Hunter, and say, "Want to get out of here? Go somewhere?"

Chapter Eighteen

The message on the home phone stops me cold. It's Ma. She called while I was at the beach and said she'd try back, although she didn't say when. Her voice is familiar, but distant.

I collapse on the couch and grip the phone to my chest. My heart is beating fast. Ma's words echo in my head, "Wanted to catch you and say hallo." It's hard to pinpoint exactly what's different in her voice. It is almost perky and light, like she's leaving a message for a stranger.

"You okay?" Hunter sits beside me. I just nod and stare at the cold stone fireplace. The stack of peat next to it is gone. "You sure? You look pale all of a sudden."

"It was Ma."

He rests his hand on my shoulder. "She okay?"

"It's the first time she's called since…" Tears feel close to the surface, but I blink them back. I turn my face toward the hall leading to the bathroom.

"Fiona told us about your mom. I'm sorry." Hunter says.

I turn the phone over in my hands. I want to listen to Ma's message again, just to hear her voice. It suddenly dawns on me that Ma usually calls my cell phone, which is always with me. But, it never rang while I was at the beach. Had she really wanted to talk to Da and not me?

Hunter says, "Anyone ever tell you that you talk with your eyes?"

His voice startles me. I scrunch my face. "No."

Hunter is looking at me intently. "You do. Horses do, too. You learn to look in their eyes and watch their body movements. It's easy to miss if you're not paying attention. Not like dogs. They yip and do as they're told. Well, most of them. No, horses have a mind of their own and don't care what people think. The problem is that they're unpredictable. Until you learn to read them."

I cross my arms and arch my brows. "So, you think you can read me?"

He says, "I'm working on it."

Outside the American students are walking back to their cottages, laughing and talking loudly. The sun filters through the streaked windows. My eyes focus on the dust suspended in the air, caught in the light. I release a deep breath. "I was beginning to think Ma would never call."

"Maybe she needed time."

"I don't know how to help her."

"Why do you think *you* need to help her?"

"Somebody has to."

"They are. At that hospital."

"They're not family."

"Maybe that's better."

"I should be there with her. Not here." Looking out the window, I say, "This isn't my home anymore."

Hunter runs his hand over the faded fabric of the couch and, in a voice barely louder than a whisper, he says, "Running away doesn't help."

"What do you know about running away?"

110

Hunter sits forward. "Maybe I thought leaving Montana would help."

"Help what?"

"Forget. Figure out what I want." He looks at the palms of his calloused hands. "But at some point I have to go home and deal with it."

"What?"

"My girlfriend. Or she *was*. We were high school sweethearts and planned to get married after I finished college. Then her friend called me at school and told me that she had an abortion and wasn't even going to tell me." His face reddens and he clenches his fists for a moment and then rubs his hands together.

"Jaysus." I turn to face him directly. His deep set eyes look sad. "What'd she say when you talked to her?"

"I didn't. Told my folks that I needed to get away and then talked Jake into coming with me to Ireland."

"Why Ireland, of all places?"

"My mother's family came from Ireland a long time ago. It seemed as good a place as any. I wanted to get as far away from her as I could."

Reaching over, I touch his muscular arm. "Maybe your girlfriend felt she couldn't talk to you. I mean, it would be hard."

Even though Hunter doesn't pull away, he doesn't acknowledge that I've moved closer. He mutters, "Not with someone you're supposed to spend your life with."

"Well, if I really didn't want to have a baby, but I knew the father would want me to, then I probably wouldn't tell him either."

"That's not fair. Or honest."

"Maybe not. But a baby changes everything."

"It doesn't have to."

"It would for me. It did for Ma."

Hunter picks at his cuticle. He seems lost in thought. I touch his smooth, thick hair. He looks at me, startled at first, and then he pulls me closer. Musk rises from his skin. As he strokes my hair, my body melts into his. Our blended, shallow breath fills the space between us. I touch his leg. He pulls me tighter. Then he leans down and kisses me. Soft. Lingering. Then hungry.

There's not much I hold back as I return his kisses.

Later, we lie together in my darkened bedroom while the night breeze tickles my exposed skin. I begin telling him about Ma. How I found her. How I was beginning to think she'd never call. Eventually everything pours out. I can't stop it. I feel comfortable telling Hunter, who will soon return home, the story I've unraveled.

I hold nothing back, except...

I don't tell Hunter that the man who talked to us at the beach was the one who saved Ma and was with me when I broke my ankle. I don't tell him why returning Ryan's call is hard.

I wait all weekend, but Ma doesn't call back. I tell myself that I should have known she wouldn't, but every part of me burned with hope that she would. I call St. Patrick's Hospital on Monday morning, and they tell me that Ma is not accepting calls or visitors, then transfer me to Dr. Mary Kilkenny. The doctor reports that Ma is making progress. She says she wasn't aware that Ma had called me, but promises to keep me updated.

Again, there's nothing to do but wait.

I have just hung up from talking to Dr. Kilkenny when there's a sharp knock on the door. It's Maeve with the twins asleep in the pram. Maeve's hair is pulled back tight and beads of sweat line her forehead. She looks past me. "Is your da home?"

"No. Why?"

"A damned pipe burst at the B&B. We got guests coming later this week."

"Call him."

"Don't you think I tried? Where is he?"

"No idea. You'll have to track him down. It's been days since I've seen him, and I'm going to be gone a day or two."

Maeve scowls. "Aren't you a help." She thrusts her double chin forward as she eyes me. "Where you off to?"

"A friend's taking me to the doctor in Castlebar and then we're driving to Galway and then, maybe to the Dingle Peninsula. He hasn't been there yet."

Maeve scoffs. "Let me guess. That American lad who is friends with Fiona's new love?"

I can't help smiling. "He's very nice."

"Just what you need." Maeve sneers and turns the pram around. "Glad you're having fun." One of the twins stirs. She reaches down and pulls the blanket up, and he snuggles in. Under her breath, she says, "Never mind me. I'll deal with everything." Then, she strolls off without a backwards glance.

Retreating indoors, I finish packing. Hunter arrives within the hour and loads my car with our bags. As we're leaving the cottage, Hunter says, "Aren't you going to leave a note?"

"No. Maeve knows." I grip the handles on my crutches and shuffle toward the door.

Hours later, at the clinic in Castlebar, the doctor proclaims my ankle fit for bearing as much of my weight as can be tolerated in the removable boot. Walking out of the clinic, I put weight down on my foot and pain shoots up my leg. Grimacing, I stop and hold onto the handrail.

Hunter holds up the crutches. "You can still use these until you get used to it."

"I'm fine." My tone is gruff. I wait a few seconds. My breath steadies and the pain ebbs. Then, standing upright and taking small steps, I limp to the car.

Hunter holds the door while I get into the passenger seat. On our way to Galway, I point out things of interest, and when we arrive, I direct him to one of my favorite places on the waterfront for a late afternoon lunch. The barman waves as we slide into a corner booth in the nearly empty pub.

My eyes adjust to the dark interior. Light filters in through the front window as we look at the menus. We each order a pint of Guinness, and later, fish and chips.

As we wait for our food, we make small talk about the antiques hanging from the ceiling and the pieces of memorabilia covering every inch of wall space in the musty pub. A man with grey, wispy hair peeking out of his tweed cap stops at our table, tips his cap, and says to me with a toothless grin, "Hello, gorgeous." He winks and then shuffles to the bar.

Hunter smiles. "You seem to have a way with men."

"Apparently so." I sip my stout. It glides easily down my parched throat.

Hunter reaches over and wipes foam from my lip. "There. Now you're perfectly gorgeous."

I feel my face flush and notice his hands resting on the table. Large. Calloused.

"What exactly do you do in Montana with horses?" I ask.

"The typical things. Feed them. Ride them. Work with the guests."

"Guests?"

"It's a guest ranch. People—families mostly—come to experience horseback riding and hiking in the mountains. Been in the family for generations."

"You'll work there after school?"

"Someone has to." Hunter grows quiet. I'm about to ask him more about the ranch when he blurts out, "I've been thinking about something you said. About your mom."

"Oh?" I suspend the glass in front of my mouth.

"Well, you said that the Walters guy told you that he and your mother had a relationship when she was a student, but he was married. Do you know when their relationship ended? I mean, could he be your dad?"

"Hell, I dunno." I drain my stout and push the glass away. "I've wondered, but couldn't bring myself to ask. It's all so feckin' unbelievable. How can this be my life?"

The server brings the fish and chips with peas and a bottle of vinegar. She asks if we are ready for another jar. We both nod and she goes off to get it. For a while neither of us says anything. A group barges into the pub, laughing and talking loudly. The musty air envelops me. Hunter grabs my hand and says, "Don't you need to know the truth."

After we leave the pub, we linger around the waterfront for the rest of the afternoon and evening. A light mist falls. My mind stews over all that Hunter said. I barely know where we are even though I've been to Galway more times than I can count.

We stop often so I can sit and rest. Still, I refuse to go back to using crutches. Instead, I lie and say it's not too bad and that the boot just takes getting used to. Finally, after a late dinner at a pub with loud music, I admit that I'm not up for driving and spending time on Dingle Peninsula the next day. I'd rather go home, where I can prop my leg and take something for the pulsating pain. Hunter agrees, and we walk back to the car.

Just past Galway in the direction of Louisburgh, a few large drops of rain splatter on the windshield, and then a steady drumbeat on the roof. Soon the wipers can't keep up with the rain pelting the windshield and making the road barely visible. A wave of exhaustion washes over me. My eyes grow heavy as I listen to the wipers swishing. I drift to sleep. When I wake up, we are entering Louisburgh.

The streets are empty except for a few parked cars. In the shops and in the flats above the pubs, all the windows are dark. Our headlights funnel light toward the holiday cottages. A few still have lights on, but our cottage is completely dark. Because the outside light above the door is turned off, Hunter leaves the headlights on so we can see our way inside.

Pulling up the collar of my jacket to cover my face, I lower my head as I walk to the cottage without crutches. The pain in my ankle slows me down. The stone path, polished with the heavy rain, is slippery and the boot has little traction. By the time I reach the door, I'm drenched. Water cascades from my hair onto my face. I fumble for the key, unlock the door, and push inside with Hunter right behind me. One of Da's boots lies in the entryway. Hunter kicks it aside.

The only light in the cottage glows from the fireplace across the room. The air smells of peat and cigar smoke. I'm trying to take off my soaked jacket when I hear Da's snoring. It's not coming from his bedroom. It's close, like he's on the couch. Then I see a movement in the shadows and my body turns ice cold. Someone's on the floor. Crouched. Like an animal.

I feel around on the wall for the light switch and flip it on. Staring at me from across the room is Paddy, wide-eyed, on his knees. He's wearing only his undershirt and socks. Grabbing a magazine to cover his crotch, he lunges for his trousers which are tossed over the back of a chair, yanks them down, and scrambles to put them on.

Hunter says, "Shit, man. What the fuck?" He reaches for me and tries pulling me in close so I can't see anymore. But, I pull back. I have to look. I have to see.

Paddy's got his pants and shirt on now. He's shaking Da, who's passed out naked on the floor.

Chapter Nineteen

Maeve's face bears a crease from the pillow and her hair stands on end when she answers the door in a housecoat that could have been my grandma's. "What the hell are you doing here?" She doesn't open the door more than a crack even though the rain is assaulting my face.

"I've got nowhere else to go," I say, pushing past her and hobbling to the kitchen. Hunter follows me into the warm B&B, dripping water onto the polished wood floor.

Maeve says, "He'll not be staying."

"I never said he was," I say, and lower myself onto a chair at the kitchen table.

Hunter sets my car keys and bag on the table. "You're sure you'll be okay?" he asks.

I shrug and peel off my soaked jacket.

He leans down, kisses my cheek, and whispers, "I'll see you tomorrow." He walks out the door to return to the place that he and Jake have been staying in down the street.

Maeve slams the door and returns to the kitchen. On the counter, laid out for breakfast, are stacked plates, cups, and saucers, and a platter of scones covered in plastic. Standing with her legs widely planted, and her arms resting on her belly, she says, "Are you going to tell me what is so bloody important that you had to come here at three in the feckin' morning?"

"I can't," I say, rocking and hugging myself.

"You're mental. Go to your granda's. No one's there. You and your boyfriend could have a grand time and not disturb the precious little sleep I'll get."

"I need to be here," I say. "With you."

"So I'm your new best friend? Saints be praised! Lucky me," Maeve huffs over to the sink, fills the teakettle, and rummages for a hand towel in the drawer. She tosses it at me. "Here. Don't drip on the floor. I just cleaned it."

I wrap the towel around my hair. My wet clothes cling to my body. I get up and limp to the hall closet, where I've stashed an extra pair of trousers and a sweater, and go into the bathroom to change. When I come back, Maeve's sitting at the table sipping tea. There's a steaming cup at my place.

The tea is strong, smooth and sweet. It goes down easily.

Maeve stares at me. "So I'm to read your mind?"

I turn away from Maeve's icy glare.

"Lovely. Well, then, let me give you some advice." Maeve leans forward on her fleshy arms and says, "Quit feeling so bloody sorry for yourself. Whatever it is that has you here with me and not with people who actually give a shite, is not my concern."

I start to say something but Maeve holds her hands up and stops me. "Deal with it. Whatever it is. Stop expecting someone else to do it for you."

Maeve drains her tea and points her finger at me. "And stop thinking some dim-witted man will make it alright. They're more bloody trouble than they're worth." She hoists herself up from the table and shuffles in her slippers to the

119

living room, to the couch, which is her bed.

I sit at the table for hours and try to make sense of everything that has happened. But, I can't. Nothing is as it has seemed. Anger swells. I want to pound the table and scream. It takes everything I have to hold it together. I don't dare wake Maeve or the guests. For the first time, I have no home and no place to go. I'm alone. I feel powerless. Tears flow until there are no more.

~

The sky finally lightens although the sun is not shining. Upstairs, the guests' feet clomp across the wooden floorboards. I hear Maeve stirring in the next room. I wait. When Maeve finally comes into the kitchen, she is dressed with her hair neatly combed. I stand up. She brushes past me and goes to the refrigerator.

I say, "I've decided to go to Dublin." I drape my damp coat over my arm and sling my bag over my shoulder. "To try and help Ma."

Maeve takes out a carton of eggs and starts cracking them into a bowl.

"I'm not coming back," I say and stand up straighter.

Maeve turns to me. "Leave if you want. Stay if you want." She reaches for the milk. "I don't care. Just let me work."

As I push the chair back to the table, it scrapes the linoleum. "Right. Well, thanks. You take care, too. What with those babies and Bobby."

"I'll be fine. Don't mind me." Maeve takes a deep breath, beats the eggs faster, and doesn't look up as I walk out the door.

Outside, a fine mist tickles my face. The sun is trying to

peek out. The hills, with their varying shades of green, glisten. I start the engine and drive down toward the cottages. My stomach knots when I see Da's car parked along the street in front of Paddy's pub.

When I reach the cottage that used to feel like home, I shower, dress, and start packing. My heart beats rapidly as I inventory what to take and what to leave behind.

Digging into the bottom of my topmost dresser drawer, I grab the money that I've stashed along with my bank card. Ma's wedding ring is still on top of the dresser. I slip it onto my pinkie and haul out a suitcase from under my bed. It fills quickly as I toss in clothes, boots, trainers, socks and underwear. There's not enough room to cram all my things in, so I go to the hall closet to get Ma's large suitcase. It is hidden in back behind the heavy coats. I wheel it back to my room, flop it onto the bed, and open it.

The canvas suitcase looks new despite a layer of dust. It's lined with compartments. One section bulges. Unzipping it, I find my soft-sided baby book. My fingers touch the pink satin cover. It smells like baby powder. I flip through the pages, brushing my fingertips over each page. Ma's perfect writing meticulously details my early years. In an envelope are locks of wispy red hair and baby teeth.

Just as I'm closing the book, Ma's passport falls out, along with a wad of money bound by a rubber band. I have no idea how much is there, but it's a lot. I open the passport. It's long expired. Ma looks at the camera blankly with her small, expressionless eyes. Her thin lips form a straight line as her black, flat hair frames her narrow face.

I put the baby book, passport, and money back into the compartment. As I do, my hand brushes across a plastic bag tucked deep into the corner. I see strands of dark hair inside it. I have to look closely to see them. Not my hair. It's too dark. And it's too red to be Ma's hair. A strong wind rattles the windows. Looking up, I see the clouds rolling in. I fold the bag back up and tuck it into the compartment.

I finish packing my things and go down the hall to my parents' room to see if there's anything I should take to Ma.

Da's clothes are strewn all over the floor. I open Ma's closet. Her clothes are on metal hangers and grouped by color. They barely fill the small closet. I touch a sweater with frayed edges that Ma wore most days. It's the color of ash. I hold it to my nose, inhaling deeply. Her scent lingers. It's the perfume I gave her. My throat tightens, and I can't swallow. I consider taking the sweater with me, but don't. I leave all her things behind except for the ring and the items I found in her suitcase.

After loading the car, I stand outside the cottage looking toward Clew Bay. Gathering clouds block the sun. Looking out at the restless water, I hold my thick hair back from the wind and inhale the salty air. Even though I've longed for more, I never saw myself leaving this way.

I never saw myself without a home. I never saw myself without a family.

Getting into the car, I drive the short distance to the school I left two years ago. Mrs. McCune, the receptionist, peers over her thick eyeglasses and greets me as I come through the office door. "Good day, Eliza." She puts down a stack of papers and rests her twisted, arthritic hands on them. "Ah, the leg is still bothering you, I see."

"It's better," I say.

"And your ma?" Mrs. McCune folds her hands as in prayer and says, "Shame she's locked away like that."

I cringe. "It's a hospital, not a prison." My tone is sharp and cold. I lean over the counter. "I need some information. Ma went to school with a girl named Linda. I want to know her last name and where she is. If you know."

Mrs. McCune's blue-veined hand fondles the thin, loose skin on her face. "The only Linda that I know who might have been in your ma's year was Linda Gallagan. Went off to London to study music, I think."

"That sounds right," I say.

"Let me check." Mrs. McCune peers at the computer screen. "I think she got married, though. Linda's parents moved to Limerick years ago, and I lost touch. I don't recall Linda's new name. My memory's not what it used to be."

I shift my weight. My ankle is starting to throb and burn.

Finally she looks up. "Ah, here it is. Linda Gallagan. Married Ian Graham." She looks back at the screen, her pointy nose just inches away. "She lives in Dublin and works at the National Performing Arts School. Aye, she did do well." Mrs. McCune shakes her head. "She and your ma were the oddest pair."

"What do you mean?"

"Well, dear. Your ma never did much, did she? A fine mother, yes. Don't take this wrong, but with the means and so little drive, I always felt badly for your grandparents. Such a shame that she didn't do more with her life. And now…"

A forced smile creeps across my face. "You've been your typical helpful self. Thank you."

Mrs. McCune flutters her spindly arms. "Of course, dear. Tell your mother everyone at the women's circle at church is praying for her."

I say I'll do that even though I know I won't.

Chapter Twenty

Driving toward the center of town, I see Fiona strutting down the street in her skinny jeans and snug sweater. She's looking down at her phone. When I pull up beside her, she jumps and nearly collides with the steel kegs lining the path.

A smile spreads across Fiona's face when I get out of my car, but then she pouts and crosses her arms over her full cleavage. "I have to hear about you and Hunter from him?"

"There's not been much to say."

Fiona smirks. "That's not true. You've been spending a lot of time together. Well done!"

"He's nice." I kick aside a piece of rubbish. "He's been a friend these past few days."

"A *very* good friend from what I hear."

"He's been better than some." My tone is harsher than I intend but don't regret.

"Now don't go biting my head off again. Since you've been off the drink, you've been a puss face. You need some craic."

"Did it ever occur to you that I might have things going on in my life?" Fiona tilts her head up at me with a puzzled expression. I say, "No, you've been too busy with Jake to give a rat's ass about me."

Fiona puts her hands on her narrow hips. "All you do is sit around and mope."

I square my shoulders and take a deep breath. "Well, I'm not now. I'm off."

"Off? But, you and Hunter..."

"He's nice and helped me a lot. But, he's going back to the States."

"Not for awhile." Fiona's tone is shrill. "He said last night after he dropped you off that he was going to extend his ticket. To spend more time with you." Fiona touches my arm. "He *really* likes you. I can tell."

I say, "There's nothing here for me. I need to leave." I hug my bag closer.

Fiona glances at the two suitcases lying on the back seat of my car next to the crutches. She says softly, "But you'll be back, yeah?"

I shake my head. "I don't think so."

Fiona holds her arms out like a child. She feels small and fragile, like a bird I might crush.

"I know you. You'll be back." Fiona's voice cracks. "This is your home."

I pull away. Looking into Fiona's makeup-smeared face, I say, "It was." I smile weakly, then turn to leave. The wind blowing off Clew Bay carries the scent of spring.

Fiona starts to say something, but I get into my car and shut the door. The windows are up. It takes everything I have not to dissolve into a puddle of tears.

All I want to do is leave. No more goodbyes. I'm grateful Da and Paddy aren't outside. There's so much to say, and yet I have no words. Not now.

The only person I really need to see before I leave is pedaling his bicycle toward home.

Mr. Walters is lifting Johnny out of the basket when I pull up. He looks surprised to see me as I walk toward him. Looking at my boot, he says, "Well, you've come a long way."

I ignore Johnny jumping on my trousers and say, "I'd like to talk to you, if you have time."

He waves me in. "Time is all I have."

I follow Mr. Walters up the path toward the door. Inside, the curtains remain shut. There's a light on over the sink. Mr. Walters walks to the stove, grabs the kettle and fills it with water. Then he opens a cupboard. It is bare except for some canned goods and seasonings. He stands there awhile before saying, "I've nothing to offer you except tea."

"I just want answers. The truth. Then I'll be on my way."

He pulls aside the curtain of the window above the sink. The sky is darkening. Then he turns his craggy face toward me. "The truth isn't always better."

"Yes, it is." My voice is strong. I pull out a chair and sit down. "I want to know why Ma married Da. I want to know who my father is." I fix my eyes on him.

His shoulders droop as he lowers himself into a chair. He sighs. "I told you that we couldn't marry. Divorce was never an option." He folds his gnarled hands. "It wasn't then, nor is it now." Mr. Walters picks at his tobacco-stained fingernail. I wait. Then he says, "When Annie found out she was pregnant, Seamus offered to marry her." The kettle starts whistling. As Mr. Walters gets up to make tea, he says, "It was perfect for all of us."

I persist. "You told me you've known Da since he was a

126

boy and that you probably know him better than most people. What did you mean by that?"

Mr. Walters sets the cups of tea down on the table. His milky eyes lock with mine. I maintain my gaze. He looks down as he lights his cigar. He says, "Let's just say I always knew he and Paddy had a *special* relationship. They were altar boys together. Inseparable from Father and then from each other in school." His words linger like the smoke lofting toward the ceiling. "To this day, in fact."

"I don't get it. Why would Ma marry him?"

"Seamus found Annie in a very difficult situation and helped make it right. It was convenient. For both of them. He could be the doting husband and father and no one needed to know his secret. She had someone who could marry her."

"Did Ma know? About Da?"

"Not at first. Later. Though she didn't want much to do with me by then. Or anyone."

"Did she tell you about that night in the pasture? About what happened? I mean, who..."

"She only told me that she was drinking with Seamus and Paddy. She got sick and Paddy offered to walk her home. She said she didn't recall what happened between her and Paddy. The next thing she remembered, she was waking up in the pasture and Seamus was there."

"Wait—*Paddy*? He could be my father?"

"Hell if I know. She said she and Seamus *got close* around this time."

The cigar smoke whirls, then evaporates. Its familiar scent lingers between us.

Mr. Walters gets up, his back hunched, and carries his

cup to the counter. The smell of soggy cereal and sour milk waft from the sink. He gazes out the window. Drops of rain start spattering the pane.

Keeping his back to me, Mr. Walters says, "Annie isn't the girl I knew. Not anymore. She changed." He turns and looks at me with moist eyes. "She didn't understand how I couldn't leave my wife. Until she had a daughter."

Rain starts drumming the roof. Slow. Steady. Mr. Walters's voice is soft as he says, "Don't you want to ask me? Don't you want to know if I'm your father?"

Despite wondering, his words send shivers down my spine. Outside, the wind churns.

Mr. Walters's chest heaves. "I thought I was for years, but now I wonder if Annie even knows. Maybe she did it on purpose? Sleep with all of us and tell none of us. She was going to have the baby. That's all that mattered to her." His lined eyes close. "In the end, it was always just you that mattered."

Rain slams the window. Mr. Walters goes over to the stand near the door and grabs an umbrella and rests it beside the door. "You're going to need this. Take it when you let yourself out." Then he whistles for Johnny, shuffles down the hall and shuts the door.

Chapter Twenty-One

After Mr. Walters shuts his door, leaving me alone and sitting there with more questions than answers, I gather my bag, limp to the door, and grab the umbrella. Using it as a shield, I put my head down and try to get to the car without losing my footing on the slick, uneven path.

Through the rapid swishes of the wipers, I try to see a few feet in front of me. All the feelings I've stuffed deep inside feel like they are going to erupt.

The windows are fogging up. I can't breathe. The hollowness and sadness I felt earlier is replaced with anger. Toward Da. Toward Paddy. Toward Mr. Walters. And toward Ma.

The wind roars. I can barely hear myself think. Does Ma even know who my father is? How will I ever know what really happened to Ma that night in the pasture? Even though Ma left that phone message four days ago, she has not returned any of my calls. Even if she did call me, would I ask these questions of her?

Do I really want to know the truth?

Hunching over the wheel, I follow the winding road out of town, gripping the wheel tighter as the rain comes down harder. My hands are numb.

The question that haunts me the most: If I mattered so

much to Ma, then why did she want to end her life and leave me? Why'd she leave me alone with the memory of her bathing in her own blood?

The wipers can't keep up. It's a solid sheet of grey. The only thing clear: My parents' secrets are now mine.

My shoulder muscles burn, and my ankle throbs. Rounding the corner, there's a sheep in the center of the road. I swerve sharply to the right to avoid hitting it, then crank the wheel back to stop skidding. The car spins around and leaves the road. Then it stops. My heart pounds. I put the car in park and check the rearview mirror for cars. There are no lights from either direction. I try catching my breath.

Wiping my face, I put the car in gear. The wheels only spin as rain pounds the windows. Slapping the wheel with my hand, I try to think what to do. Pulling my phone from my bag, I check the GPS. I'm only a few kilometers from Westport. I look up the number for roadside service and call for help. They tell me it could be up to two hours. There's no choice but to wait. I turn on the emergency flashers and sink into the seat. The windows fog up. While I wait, all the questions spin in my mind again. More than two hours pass before I see the tow truck's yellow flashing lights.

After getting hooked up and pulled back onto the road, I follow the truck's taillights into Westport. At the center of town on James Street is the Clew Bay Hotel. I've never been inside it before. Fiona and I only walked by it on the way to the nearby pubs. It costs more than I'd like to spend on a night's lodging, but there's an open parking spot in front. All I care about is getting out of the car and out of my wet clothes.

After paying for a night's stay, I drag my suitcase through

the newly remodeled lobby and take the elevator to the second floor. The room is at the end of the hall and overlooks the street. It smells like fresh paint and new carpet. After stripping off my wet clothes, I burrow beneath the down comforter, close my eyes and listen to the relentless rain. Soon I fall into a deep sleep.

My cell phone rings, jarring me awake. I let it go into voicemail. A dim light illuminates the far end of the room. Everything is still. No rain. No traffic sounds. No sounds from neighboring rooms. Stretching like a cat, I will myself to get up only because I have to pee.

Under the fluorescent lights in the bathroom, my skin looks blotchy. My eyes are puffy and red, and my hair is a wild mane, tangled and standing on end. Cranking the faucet, I fill the tub, step into the warm water, and submerge myself in floral-scented bubbles.

When I emerge, wrapped in the hotel's oversized, fluffy robe, I check my messages. Fiona called. I ring her back.

"You're not going to believe this." Fiona's voice blares into the phone. "Jake's leaving with Hunter. Going back to the States."

"Brutal." I let myself relax into the mound of pillows on the bed.

"The worst is he now tells me he has a fiancée back home." There's the sound of a cabinet slamming shut. "The prick."

"He tells you this now?"

"Hunter said he had to come clean and tell me." In the background there's the sound of ice clinking in a glass. "Well, he can kiss my arse."

"You'll find someone else."

"You're bloody right I will." Fiona gulps something. "You need to come home. I don't want to be alone right now."

"I can't." I don't tell Fiona that I'm only twenty minutes away.

"But, I *need* you!" she whines.

"You'll be fine without me. I'll call when I'm settled. You can visit sometime."

"I need you *now*." Fiona's voice is still whiney but softer.

I sit up and hug the pillow. "Well, I've got to go now. Sorry." I hang up before Fiona can squeeze in another word. I cover my face with the pillow and feel my body sink into the bed.

I lay there debating whether I should go back to Louisburgh, just to make sure Fiona is going to be alright. But I know I can't go back. Not yet. Maybe never.

There's one thing I have to do before leaving for Dublin tomorrow. I call the number stored in my phone.

"Ryan here."

"Oh, hallo. This is Eliza."

"Eliza. Splendid to hear your voice. How are you?"

My voice sounds higher than normal and quite perky. "Grand. I wanted to make arrangements to bring your crutches by. Perhaps tomorrow on my way out of town?"

"You're driving through Westport tomorrow?"

"I'm actually here. At the Clew Bay Hotel. I spent the day here after I got stranded with the rain. I'll be going to Dublin in the morning. Can I bring the crutches by the clinic then?"

"You're here?"

"Just for the night."

"Well, then, I can save you the trip. Have you eaten yet?"

I glance at the clock. It's nearly six o'clock. "Well, no, but..."

"Excellent. We can eat dinner at the restaurant there. Say in an hour?"

"Umm." I can't think of an excuse. "Lovely."

We hang up. I touch my puffy eyes and scramble out of bed to get a cold washcloth to put on them. Then I dig through my suitcase for my makeup and something presentable to wear. My footwear choices are limited. Finally I settle on a cashmere cardigan and boot-cut jeans.

Ryan is waiting for me in the lobby when I get off the elevator. He's holding a small bouquet of flowers. When he sees me, his eyes widen. He smiles and says, "I'll be damned."

I feel myself blush. He hands me the flowers and kisses my cheek. Then, he takes my elbow and guides me to the restaurant.

The barman is watching the rugby match on the big screen and talking to an elderly man clutching his stout. Unlike at Paddy's pub, the stools are leather and the bar a polished, dark granite. We find a table by the front window. Soon, a server brings us menus. After contemplating our drink order, we agree on the house red wine.

We make small talk, mostly about the dreadful weather and lambing that has kept Ryan busy, along with his training. The server arrives, uncorks the wine, and pours us each a glass. It goes down smoothly. My stomach rumbles as we place our food order.

The bouquet rests on the corner of the table. I touch one of the lilies. "Thanks for these."

"I hope your boyfriend doesn't want to beat me up, but I still feel bad about your leg."

"Boyfriend?"

"The guy I saw you with on the beach."

"Oh, him." I avoid his eyes. "He's just a tourist. An American. He's not my boyfriend."

A smile spreads over Ryan's freckled face. He lifts the wine bottle and refills my glass. I look out the large-paned window. Puddles glisten under the streetlights. People walk by with closed umbrellas. A silence lingers between us like the morning mist. As he touches my fingers, he says, "I've been thinking of you."

I pull my hand back and put it on my lap. "That right?" I take a long sip of wine. It warms my throat. My cheeks feel flush. "How's Alex?"

Ryan shrugs. "Okay, I guess. Moving to New York. Got a modeling job." He folds his hands on the table. "I'll miss her."

"No doubt," I say. I break off a piece of bread, slather it with butter and take an interest in looking around the empty restaurant.

"You okay?"

I stuff the bread into my mouth. "Grand."

"Did I say or do something wrong?"

"No. I'm just tired. And hungry." I look around for the server to bring our food. I offer Ryan the bread basket, but he shakes his head. I take another piece and ask, "How's your training for the tri going?"

"Excellent." He runs his hands through his curly hair. "I wish you could do it, too."

"There'll be others," I say, rotating my stiff ankle.

"Right." Ryan leans forward and tries to touch my hand again, but I pull it away. He just stares at me.

The server arrives with our salad. Ryan sprinkles his with lemon while I coat mine with dressing. I take a bite. "Will you and Alex try to visit each other often?"

He shakes his head. "Probably not. I'll get another flatmate."

"It'll be hard to replace her in your life."

"Not really. I mean, she's been great, and we've known each other since university, but we didn't do much or see each other often. Mostly she stayed with her boyfriend."

My mouth hangs open. "Boyfriend?"

"Plays rugby for the union team. Nice lad."

"Oh, I just assumed..."

Ryan laughs. "Alex likes *real* athletes."

My breath escapes and I smile. He refills my glass and motions to the server to bring another bottle. This time I don't pull my hand away when he reaches for it. His hands are smooth and strong.

He leans forward. "So where were you on your way to?"

"Dublin. To see Ma."

"Oh, she'll see you now? Excellent." He squeezes my hand.

"Well, I don't know. I hope so."

The server returns with another bottle of wine. After uncorking it, she fills our glasses and then goes to check on our food. Ryan brushes his fingertips over my arm. His dark brown eyes meet mine. "Maybe we can spend some time together when you get back."

Shivers snake through my body. "I'll not be back. Not to Louisburgh."

He raises his eyebrows.

"There's a lot that's happened since I saw you last. Too much. Let's just say that I have no bloody clue who my da is."

Ryan's back straightens, and he shakes his head. "I still can't believe my uncle and your ma. It's a good thing I've not seen him." His voice is brittle and hard.

"It's complicated. Not just with him, but with Da. With Paddy."

Ryan prods gently until piece by piece it all unravels. Except the piece about finding Da with Paddy. That I can't tell. His slender fingers intertwine with mine. "So now what are you going to do?"

"That's what I'm trying to figure out. Do I want to know who my da really is? A drunk. A rapist. Or a predator. Nice choices."

"They're more than that. And less, too." Ryan leans closer. The fine lines around his eyes deepen. He says, "You'll be okay, you know."

Our faces are nearly touching. His breath is sweet and he carries on his clothes the faint aroma of citrus. My pulse is racing. Our lips meet. Soft. Warm.

Then the server, who had disappeared earlier, appears with our salmon and almond green beans. We release hands. The space between us widens, and the air cools. For a time neither of us says anything as we eat our food. There's a quiet buzz of conversation from the tables next to us, as more people have come into the restaurant.

My thoughts come back to what I don't know. What I might never know. I say, "I thought of getting one of those paternity tests. I've heard you can order them online."

Ryan butters a roll. "I'm not sure how reliable they are. You can also spend a bit more and have it done properly."

"I don't have that much money."

"Get *them* to pay."

"Your uncle? He said he wondered but will he actually agree to a test now?" I drain the last of the wine in my glass.

"You have some bargaining power." When I cock my head,

Ryan explains. "A teacher involved in a relationship with a student. Granted, it was a long time ago. But dear uncle does care about his fine reputation as beloved music teacher, despite what he might let on."

I chew my food and nod. I think about the time I spent at Mr. Walters's when I found the yearbooks in the drawer, and the envelope that I never opened but simply put back. After folding my napkin on the table, I say, "There's a lot to think about. And to do."

Ryan orders two Irish coffees and tells the server to bring him the tab. All of a sudden, he digs out his phone. "Before I forget. I just remembered that I know someone at the hospital in Castlebar who could help get you set up with the paternity testing. I wonder if I have his number here."

I take his phone and set it down on the table. He looks at me with a puzzled expression. I reach up and touch his rosy cheek. My body is tingling. The room is spinning slightly. I catch Ryan glancing at my respectable cleavage in the cashmere cardigan. My heart beats faster. Leaning forward, he kisses my parted lips.

I whisper, "It can wait."

Chapter Twenty-Two

Birds chirp outside and the sun shines through the sheer curtains as Ryan, already dressed, kisses my neck. "Morning, love," he whispers. He takes the sheet, which is draped over my hip, pulls it up and tucks it under my chin.

I pull him towards me and hold him tight. "First you keep me up all night, and then you wake me at the crack of dawn."

"It's nearly eight o'clock. I've got to shower and get ready for work." He brushes my hair out of my face, his breath still sweet with wine. "The offer to stay at my flat is open. Not only do I make a deadly seafood fettuccine, I can be irresistible, as well." He winks.

"You think highly of yourself," I tease.

"You'll come?" His impish smile spreads freckles across his face.

I release him and shrug. "Unless I get a better offer."

He smiles and gets up. "I'll text you the address." As he's putting on his jacket, he snaps his fingers as he remembers something. "Oh, and I'll call that person at the hospital who might know about the paternity testing options." Then he bends down and kisses me one more time, checks to make sure he has his phone, and leaves.

I lay there awhile but can't fall back to sleep. My mouth is dry and I have no appetite for food, only water.

I get my laptop and, after connecting to the Internet, search Linda Graham's name. Most recent postings highlight her teaching at the Performing Arts School in Dublin. Older ones commend her singing and theatrical performances. There's a picture of her. While it looks like it was taken some time back, Linda doesn't look like someone who would be friends with Ma. She looks proud, confident and important. There's no answer when I call the number for the Performing Arts School. I hang up without leaving a message.

Then I ring Fiona, who growls, "Who the fuck is calling me this early?"

"Your best friend. Have you removed my number from your phone already so you didn't know who is calling?"

"Jaysus, Eliza, you know I hate mornings."

"Then why answer?"

"The bloody phone was by my ear."

"I need you to do something for me."

It takes a while before Fiona is fully awake, but she agrees to help me when I explain what I need her to do. I have her repeat back to me the instructions I gave her, and we agree to meet in the restaurant here in the hotel around four o'clock, even though I'm checking out later this morning.

Ryan calls shortly before ten o'clock. "Here's the deal with the paternity testing. Each person gives a blood sample at the hospital in Castlebar, and they send it to the testing center in Dublin. Or there's the option of going directly to Dublin. The results are back in about a week. You're right, there are home kits, but they aren't as reliable."

"First I have to convince them to do it."

139

"You'll let me know if you need help with my uncle?"

"I think I can manage."

"Then I'll see you for dinner at my flat? Six o'clock?"

"Lovely."

"I promise to be a perfect gentleman."

"Then I might not come," I say with a smile, and hang up.

After showering, I check out of the hotel and drive to the hospital in Castlebar. There they draw blood and give me the release forms and instructions to give to Da, Paddy, and Mr. Walters.

During the drive to Louisburgh, I run through what I'll say to each of them. It's close to two o'clock when I park along the narrow street in the town square. People and dogs amble by, and I greet them by name, making small talk with a few about the lovely weather that has finally arrived. Looking down the street, I see Da's car parked in front of Paddy's pub.

The sun, high in the sky, burns my eyes, so I put on my sunglasses and walk the few streets to Mr. Walters's house. He's outside with Johnny in his tiny yard. When I open the gate, he cocks his head at me for a moment, then bends down and pulls out a handful of weeds. Under his breath, he mutters, "Heard you left. Couldn't stay away after all?"

"There are a few things to wrap up. I'm packed and heading to Dublin soon." I close the creaky gate. "I need to talk to you about something."

"Is that right? Be quick. I have things to do." He keeps weeding.

"I want you to take a paternity test."

He brushes the dirt from his gnarled hands. "You think that will fix everything?"

"It's better than not knowing."

"I wouldn't be so sure." He straightens up and looks at me over his thick glasses. "I suggested this to your mother, and she'd hear nothing of it. Insisted Seamus was the father."

I thrust the papers at him. "*I* need to know."

He shakes his head and says, "Annie might be right. Sometimes the truth serves no purpose. Seamus raised you. I suppose you turned out fine enough in spite of that. I'll not do any testing."

"You have to." My voice cracks.

"No. I don't."

"If you don't, then I'll have no choice but to…"

"To what?" Mr. Walters says, "You can't force me to do anything."

I take off my sunglasses and look Mr. Walters in the eye. "Don't you think the headmaster might find your past trysts with a student troublesome?"

"You wouldn't do that. It'd destroy your mother."

"Isn't it too late for that?"

Mr. Walters mutters, "She loved me and wanted to be with me."

I raise my voice and say, "You took advantage of her. She trusted you. Even if she wanted a relationship, you were much older and you could have stopped it. Good God, you were married, too!"

He turns to face me. "You won't say anything."

I just stare at him.

Mr. Walters looks away. "She was a consenting adult by then. It doesn't matter what happened before. It was a long time ago."

"Not everyone may see it that way."

As I hold Mr. Walters's gaze and the papers, my breath quickens but my resolve doesn't waver even though my hand trembles.

After what seems an eternity, he snarls, "Give me the damn papers." He snatches them from my hands. Then he whistles for Johnny who trails him into the house. The door slams shut.

My legs feel weak as I stand tall looking at the closed door. I can hear Johnny barking inside. Turning, I swallow the sour taste in my mouth, taking deep breaths to still my pounding heart.

Passing the grocery, I see that Fiona's car, usually parked in front, is gone.

I enter Paddy's pub. Inside is Da, slumped alone at the bar with his hair standing on end and his wrinkled shirt hanging over his trousers. He doesn't look up until I'm standing next to the bar. Seeing me, he knocks the stool over backwards as he stands up to hug me. As usual, he reeks of cigar smoke and stale whiskey. He grips me tightly and buries his head. "Eliza, baby, I didn't know where you went."

I pull back, looking around the empty, dark pub. "I need to talk to you. Paddy, too."

"He's in back talking on the phone." Da runs his hand over his grey stubble. "You had me worried half to death leaving. Taking your things, too. And in that bloody rain."

I cross my arms. "I'm not staying."

His face drops and his eyes water. "But where will you go? This is your home."

"Not anymore." I slip behind the bar and pour myself a Diet Coke. Without meeting his eyes, I say, "Things have changed. You know that."

Da rights and remounts the stool. He clutches his glass with both hands. Looking down, he mutters, barely louder than a whisper, "I'm so sorry you...um...saw..."

From behind the bar, I look at the framed pictures of Da and Paddy in their rugby uniforms on the far wall. Taking a deep breath, I ask, "How long? With Paddy."

Da takes a big swallow and stares into the empty glass.

"I want to know." I run my hand along the polished wood on which I did my homework.

"A daughter should never find her da like that." Tears flow down his ruddy cheeks.

"How long?"

Da sighs. "Since school." His voice lowers. "Off and on. We both tried to stop, but couldn't. We just kept coming back to each other."

"Did Ma know?"

He shakes his head. "Not at first."

"But you told me that she didn't like men."

Da shrugs his massive shoulders. "She and me were... together...a couple of times before we got married. Then a couple of times afterwards." He rubs his chafed knuckles. "It was a hard pregnancy. After you came along, she only had time for you. It suited me though. Made it easier."

"What does that mean?"

He reaches for the whiskey bottle and fills his glass. "It was hard for me to be with her. I could do it. Most of the time anyway."

"Then why did you marry her?"

"You wouldn't understand." He takes a big gulp, nearly draining the glass.

"Try me," I say.

Without looking at me, he says, "It was Paddy with your ma. In the pasture. I found his keys by her. I knew he followed her home and..." He chokes back tears and wipes his nose on his sleeve. "I talked to him the next day, and he didn't remember anything. But he didn't deny it." He looks past me to nothing in particular. "I never told your ma it was Paddy." Da fills his glass again and takes a swallow. He says, "It was Paddy's idea that I seduce her in case she was pregnant. He could never marry her."

"Why not?"

"She hated him. He liked Linda before, and it drove your ma mad. That's why we thought they might have a thing for each other." He takes another swallow. "But we never knew for sure."

Light streaks through the unwashed window. My stomach feels hollow. I take the information sheet and release form from my bag and slide them across the bar. "I want to know who my father is. You and Paddy need to go to the hospital in Castlebar and give some blood so they can send it in to test your DNA with mine."

Da starts sobbing. He buries his head in his arm. I feel like I'm watching a stranger grieve. When his sobs turn to whimpers, I say softly, "Please, enough of the secrets. Enough of the lies. If you ever loved me, do this. For me."

With his nose dripping, Da looks up. His bloodshot eyes are rimmed with tears, and he says, "I do love you. Always have. You're my daughter regardless of any damn test."

For a moment, I can't speak. I grip the bar tighter. "Get Paddy to do it, too. I don't care what you say or do to make it happen. Here's the address and the contact person." I slide the papers closer.

Da nods, grabs the papers and stuffs them into his shirt pocket without looking at them.

"And I want you both to have the lab release the information to me. I want to see it first. Understand?"

Da lowers his eyes. "Aye."

I pour the full glass of Diet Coke into the sink and walk out from behind the bar. There's the smell of a peat fire long since extinguished and ale freshly spilled. Da is slumped on the stool. I put my hand on his heaving shoulders and say, "I know that you did what you thought was right at the time. Do what's right now."

I leave quickly before he can see the tears streaming down my face.

Chapter Twenty-Three

When I arrive at the Clew Bay Hotel, Fiona is sitting on the outside patio wearing oversized sunglasses and smoking. She flaps her arms. "Darling, here!"

The people at the next table lean in and whisper while staring at Fiona, who is displaying her taste in low-cut apparel.

Fiona hugs me while holding her cigarette high. "I got it," she whispers in my ear. "No one saw me." The server brings two pints of ale that Fiona apparently ordered. She grips the glass with her manicured nails. "Good idea to meet here. No one knows us."

"I actually stayed here last night. With the rain and all." Another grey-haired couple wearing sweats and trainers joins the people at the next table. I ask, "How'd it go?"

Fiona pats her bag as her eyes dart around. "It was exciting sneaking in."

"Any problems?"

"No. It was right where you said it would be. I waited until Weird Willie left on his bike with that damn dog. I had to talk to Mrs. O'Reilly at the chemist until he was far gone."

"Did she see you go to his house? Did anyone?"

"Not a soul." Fiona lowers her voice and points her cigarette at me. "I just walked down the street minding my own business and pretended to knock on his door. I tested it, and it wasn't locked. Quiet as a bloody church mouse I was."

Fiona reaches into her bag and pulls out the manila envelope fastened with a string. "There was nothing else there except the yearbook you told me about."

I take the envelope and hold it like a fragile egg. "Did you open it?"

"That's fucking insulting. Don't you trust me?"

I narrow my eyes. "Not since Mikey."

"Kiss my arse. How many times do I have to apologize?"

I look away.

Fiona lights another cigarette and flips her hair back. "I could have looked, but I told you I wouldn't. You're worse than me mother."

Even though I'm not sure she's telling the truth, I say, "Okay. I'll believe you."

Fiona leans forward. "Jaysus, Eliza. What's inside?"

My hands are sticking to the envelope. "Dunno. I just remembered seeing it in the bedside drawer when I was staying there after the surgery. I'll look at it later."

Fiona blows smoke out the side of her mouth. "You think it's important?"

I shrug. "It's probably nothing, but for some reason it bothered me that I never looked inside. It was with the yearbook that had Ma's pictures in it." I rub my fingers over the bulging envelope.

"Let's open the bloody thing." Fiona reaches for the envelope, but I tuck it inside my bag and pull it close. She sinks into her chair and pouts. "After all that I did for you?"

"You're a love. Really. Sorry I bit your head off. But it's nothing." I lean forward. "Besides, I want to know what happened with Jake. And Hunter. How's he?"

"Who knows?" Fiona takes a long gulp of the ale. "But Jake's a can of piss. I made a holy show before they left. You should have been there."

"Wish I was. But you'll find someone else."

"Bloody right." Fiona flags the server and orders another round. "Remember that fat American staying in the cottages who bought my bra his first night here? Well, let's just say I have my bra back and didn't have to pay a thing."

"Not even one night of mourning?"

"Turns out his da is a big shot at Coca Cola. He's swimming in money and more than happy to spend it on me." Fiona flicks her ashes over the side of the table onto the path rather than into the glass ashtray. "Jake can kiss my arse."

Fiona rails on Jake, and I keep nodding while my mind drifts to the envelope. It's probably nothing, I tell myself. Just papers. He probably won't miss it. A part of me feels guilty. Then I think of Ma. I start to get warm and take off my jacket. Wrapping my hands around my glass, I listen to Fiona blather on about Jake. When I say she can do better, she flies off, recounting all his faults.

Fiona says she has to pee. After she goes inside, I take out the envelope and unwind the string. I peek inside. There are three bundles of letters and cards separated by binders.

I lift out one pack of letters. I recognize Ma's writing. I look up and don't see Fiona coming so I unfold the first one. It's not dated. Ma wrote, "It's nice having someone to share this with. I can talk to you. You listen and don't judge me. Thank you for being my friend. Annie."

The next one reads, "I've never had anyone be so kind to me before. You don't think I'm weird or treat me like a child. I hope I can be there for you if you ever need anyone to listen to you. It must be hard to listen to everyone. Thank you for being there for me. Annie."

A car speeds past, invading my lungs with a trail of dark fumes and sending me into a coughing jag. The people at the next table curse the driver. There's no more ale to wash the taste out of my mouth and no sign of the server or Fiona.

The next undated letter reads: "It must be hard being married when you're so misunderstood. Thank you for sharing your feelings. I've never had anyone tell me that they love me. Please don't think that I left because I didn't want to be with you. I just never had anyone touch me in such a tender way and I panicked. I was afraid someone would come in and see us. Next time I will be prepared. I hope to see you soon. Love, Annie."

Rapidly I flip through the other letters while peeking up to see if Fiona is coming. Most are short messages from Ma about her love and longing for Mr. Walters. I can't tell if Mr. Walters was writing notes to Ma based on what Ma wrote. It's all about her feelings for him.

The sun dips behind a cloud. I take off my sunglasses to read the last letter in this bunch. It appears to be written shortly before school ends, as Ma talks about her friends leaving for university while Granda refuses to pay for her to go. She writes: "I can't see you anymore. I need to decide what to do. I might go away. You know I want to travel and start over somewhere. Maybe this is the right time. I will always hold you dear. Love, Your Annie."

My breath lodges in my lungs, trapped.

Fiona slides into her chair. "What is it?"

Stuffing the bundled letters back, I say, "Nothing important." I refasten the envelope and stuff it into my bag as the server arrives with our ales. "I want to hear about your new love. What's his name?"

Fiona scrunches her freshly painted face. "Bloody hell. I forgot the bloke's name." She then blathers on about Jake not telling her that he was engaged.

My mind wanders to the letters as I listen to Fiona prattle about the love she lost but never really had. A text message comes in from Ryan. He's off work early and wants me to come by sooner. I mutter disparaging comments about Jake to pacify Fiona. Then, after one more drink, I tell her that I have to go.

"But we need to go out for great craic before you leave." Fiona starts gathering her things.

I set my money down. "That'd be grand, but I have to head. Told Ryan I'd meet him."

Fiona rolls her heavily coated eyes. "He's *so* dull."

"Everyone's dull compared to you." I stand up, pull on my coat, squeeze around the chairs, and hug Fiona. I promise to let her know where I end up. Even before I've made my way to the street, I hear Fiona's high-pitched voice; she's already on the phone.

My ankle feels stiff as I'm walking to the car. I clutch my bag. A part of me had doubted Mr. Walters until Ma's words confirmed the twisted reality that now was part of mine.

And now I am heading for his nephew's flat.

As I walk back to my car, I stop at a liquor store for a bottle of wine to bring to Ryan's. Across the street is the laundromat. I cast a glance. Then I stop. Through the window,

Jake's unmistakable nose, hooked and looming on his narrow face, catches my attention. Fiona had said they were leaving. Had she said they were in Westport and I missed that? Hunter's back is facing the window. There's no mistaking his broad shoulders and muscular arms.

I step behind a street lamp but it doesn't hide me. My breath is rapid, and I grip the bottle tightly. I sneak another look. Hunter is stacking folded clothing and Jake is transferring it into a duffle bag. I step forward, determined to cross the street and speak to Hunter. But what is there to say? Panicking, I scurry toward my car, hoping they haven't seen me.

When I arrive at Ryan's flat, he opens the door wearing his running shorts. "I'm afraid I thought I had time for a run when you texted that you were with Fiona and would be by later." His pale, freckled skin looks rosy. "I haven't showered yet."

His skin glistens and tastes salty when he kisses me. Immediately I'm aware of the alcohol on my breath. I wave him away. "Go ahead. I'm fine."

He says, "Make yourself at home. Relax and put your ankle up."

The sun beams through the large windows and bounces off the daffodil colored walls. A breeze filters in through an open kitchen window and circulates through the spacious flat. My hand brushes the back of the soft leather couch as I walk by.

Pictures hang on the wall bordering the flat screen television. Ryan in running shorts and a numbered racing bib, posing with other runners in front of the Roman Colosseum. Ryan playing his guitar in a pub with his mates.

Across the room, his guitar is still propped in the corner.

Fresh flowers adorn a table. On it, there's a framed picture of a woman with long, silky black hair and dark, exotic eyes. I don't know how long I've been staring at that picture when Ryan comes up behind me. I turn. He's dressed in a linen shirt and khakis. He says, "I thought you'd be resting with your ankle up."

"She's lovely."

"Yes. She was." He wipes some dust off the wooden frame. "Monique and I met when I was traveling in France. My parents thought I'd stay there." He sighs and stares at the picture. "They were right. I would have."

"What happened?"

"She got sick. Ovarian cancer. Doctors said it was too far along. So I helped her parents care for her until..." His voice softens. "We thought we'd have longer."

"I'm sorry." I touch his arm.

Ryan sighs and says, "You never know when people you love will be gone." He adjusts the picture. "That's when I came home and went back to school so I could join my da at the clinic."

"I can't imagine coming back to Ireland after living in France."

He says, "We all make choices."

"I feel like I need to take care of Ma. Except I don't know what I should do, or can do, to help her." I walk to the couch and sit down. Picking up one of the brightly-colored throw pillows, I run my fingers over the silky fabric. "So I find out who my father is. Where does that get me? And how does it help her?"

Ryan joins me. "You don't need to figure that out right now. Take one thing at a time."

I look up at his narrow face. "It's nice of you to let me stay here." With the dark eyes and cowlick, he looks nothing like his uncle.

"As long as you like." He starts kissing me, softly at first. Then harder, more urgently. I remind myself that he's related to Mr. Walters only by marriage and pull him closer.

Then I push him away. He looks confused. I smooth my hair and button my blouse. "I'm sorry. It's just...you still seem to have feelings for Monique."

Ryan tilts his head back and closes his eyes. "I'll always have feelings for her. You don't stop loving someone just because they're no longer here."

"She was so beautiful and I..."

"You're beautiful, too. And you're here." He tries pulling me closer, but I stand up and tuck my blouse into my jeans. He lets out a heavy breath. "Can't we just see where this goes?"

"I know where this is going."

"You were okay with it last night." He teases. "Quite."

"I don't need this distraction." I look toward the door. "Not now."

Ryan stands, grabs me around the waist, and says, "Maybe that's just what you need." He kisses my neck. Warm. Soft. Tempting.

"No." I turn my head and drop my arms to my side, but don't move away. "You don't get it. He's your uncle and he..."

Ryan rolls his eyes. "I'm not him." He takes my head in his hands and holds my face close to his. I can smell his sweet breath. "I didn't do anything to you. Or to her—other than try to help."

His hands cool my flushed face. I tell myself that a distraction isn't the worst thing. Just for tonight. No commitment. Like Hunter, who is on his way back home, I'll be on my way soon. I wrap my arms around his neck and kiss him hard and long. When he leads me into the bedroom, I offer no resistance.

Later that night, as Ryan sleeps next to me, I stare at the ceiling. All I can think about is Ma. How'd it start with Mr. Walters? How'd they keep it a secret? Did anyone else know? Wouldn't Ma have told Linda? Why'd she end it? What if he is my father? If so, have I been sleeping with my cousin?

I can't stay in bed any longer. It's dark in the room except for a sliver of light peeking through the crack in the curtains. Stepping over my clothes, which are scattered everywhere, I grab Ryan's robe hanging over the back of a chair. I slip it on and tiptoe to the other room.

There's no sound coming from the other flats. Even the birds are quiet. I stand by the window and stare out at the parked cars. Then I find my bag, sit on the couch, and turn on the lamp. Taking out the bundle of Ma's letters again, I read each one. Then I read them again. And again.

The words sink in, but the story's incomplete.

I dig out another bundle, which is mostly cards. It's not Ma's writing. A person named Camille signs them. In one, she laments how she misses spending time together since the end of the play. She writes in the handful of cards, none of which are dated, about how special he makes her feel.

I'm cold and I pull the robe closer as I reach for the last bundle.

There is a series of letters written by a girl named Marie. She writes about sneaking into Mr. Walters's office after school when others were gone. And about losing her virginity just before final exams. The details in each letter turn my stomach. Her last letter unleashes a torrent of anger and despair over Mr. Walters ending their relationship. I flip through the letters again. None are dated.

With the cards and letters scattered next to me, I hug my legs close. Were these girls from Ma's class as well? How many girls had Mr. Walters comforted or made to feel "special" over the years? How many others offered their virginity to him in exchange for his love?

How many other lives had he destroyed besides Ma's?

Chapter Twenty-Four

I wake up on the couch, covered with a blanket. There's a note from Ryan propped against a full glass of water on the end table asking me to call him. Stretching, I suddenly recall the letters. I sit up and frantically look around. They're heaped on the floor. Gathering them, I put them back into the envelope. When I tromp into the kitchen, the clock reads ten.

It became clear last night that I need to track down Linda. She's the only person I can think of who might help me find answers. Grabbing my phone, I call the National Performing Arts Center. She's not available, but I leave a voicemail message that I'm Annie Conroy's daughter and would like to talk to her. I don't tell her about Ma. Later I'm sitting at the table with a cup of tea and a bowl of fruit when my phone rings. Linda introduces herself.

Standing, I begin pacing. "Oh, thank you for calling back. You went to school with my mother, Annie, and—"

"How's your mother? You were just a baby when I saw you." Linda's tone is professional, but kind.

"She tried to kill herself three months ago."

"Oh, Lord! Is she...?"

"Alive, but not well. She's actually in Dublin. At St. Patrick's."

"I'm sorry. I don't know what to say. It's been so long since I've spoken to her."

"I've been trying to sort out why Ma would do this. It was so sudden. I was wondering if I could meet with you since you were such good friends with her."

"I have no idea how I can help you. It's been years since I've seen or talked to her."

"I just think if I knew more about her past, then I might understand things. Maybe why she did it." I can hear the desperation mounting in my voice. "I promise not to take too much of your time. I could meet you anywhere."

There is a long pause. "Where are you now?"

"Westport." I add quickly, "But I'm coming to Dublin soon."

A breath exhales into the receiver. "If you can be here later today, then I could meet with you. If not, it'll have to wait until I return from holiday."

"That's no problem. I can be there in four hours. Where should I meet you?"

"Come to the school. I'm getting things in order before I leave. Just ring my mobile when you arrive and I'll meet you in front. Let me give you that number."

There's no time to waste. Dublin is more than three hours away without any stops. I shower quickly and gather the few things I have in Ryan's flat, retrieve the crutches from the back seat of my car and prop them in the corner by the door, and begin the drive. The rolling hills ahead of me are brilliant green in the sun. I've been driving nearly fifteen minutes and am approaching Castlebar when it dawns on me that I haven't called Ryan yet.

The receptionist at the clinic puts me on hold. When

Ryan gets on the line, I tell him I've left for Dublin to see Ma's friend Linda. He's quiet at first. "I thought you were going to wait for the test results."

"The hospital, when I gave my sample, said I could go directly to the testing facility in Dublin. That's what I'll do now."

"What's the rush?" Ryan asks.

"You know I need to figure things out, and Linda's leaving on holiday tomorrow."

"So see her when she comes back."

"I can't wait," I tell him.

"Will it make any difference?"

My eyes fix on the car ahead of me. Its driver keeps putting on the brakes. "There's so much you don't know."

"Then tell me."

"I can't. Not now. Maybe someday. But I've got to go. Bye, love."

I don't wait for Ryan's reply. I just hang up and toss the phone onto the passenger seat and accelerate out of Castlebar, past the stone-walled pastures, under a cloudless sky.

It is early afternoon when I arrive in Dublin and find the National Performing Arts Center on Barrow Street. As I search for parking, I call Linda to let her know I'm here. People crowd the street littered with vendors peddling their wares, and the smell of pub food stirs my appetite. I stick a piece of gum into my mouth and walk the few streets to the school.

Standing at the door is a woman with ginger hair cut short. She smiles and introduces herself as Linda. She's wearing a stylish straight-lined skirt that accentuates her trim figure. "I see you found the building just fine. Please come in. We'll go to my studio." After we walk a few meters, she stops and looks at my boot. "You okay?"

"Oh, fine. I broke my ankle running down Croagh Patrick. But every day it's better."

She smiles and adjusts her pace to mine. As we twist and turn down hallways, she makes small talk about the drive. Finally, she extends her hand to usher me into the spacious, bright room. There's a desk and two chairs. "Here we are. Please have a seat."

Each wall is painted a variant shade of blue. A different word is painted on each wall: Dream; Dare; Devote; Discipline. "What do you teach?" I ask.

"Voice." Linda motions to a chair and sits in the other chair. She reaches for a plate on the desk. "Would you like a biscuit? A bottle of water?" After I take one of each, Linda sits back and crosses her well-toned legs.

"I appreciate you meeting me, especially as you get ready to leave on holiday."

"I've been just sick thinking of poor Annie since you told me about her." Linda shakes her head. Tied around her neck is a flowing, colorful scarf that matches her silk blouse. "Have you seen her?"

"No. She hasn't wanted to see me. Not yet."

"It's been years since I've talked to her. Until I saw you, I didn't feel that much older. Where does time fly?"

"It's nice to finally meet you." I take a bite of the biscuit. It crunches in my mouth.

"So your mother talked about me?" Linda's eyes are expectant.

"Actually, no. I saw your name in a school yearbook.

When I asked Da about you, he told me you and Ma were friends."

"Friends since we were wee girls." Her freckled face has only a few lines around her glossed lips.

"What was she like then?"

"Oh, shy. Insecure. She didn't make friends easily. Sometimes she got jealous, especially when I started dating. It's funny, really, that she married before I did. I could have more easily been the one to get pregnant, not her." She points her finger at me like a teacher reprimanding a student. "Not that I was easy, mind you." Linda sighs and grabs a biscuit, but doesn't take a bite. "Annie was always protective of me. Afraid I wouldn't get my homework done. Afraid I'd stay out too late drinking."

"She's like that—or was—with me, too," I say.

"She's your mother." Linda smiles. "I'll never forget seeing you right after you were born. Annie looked so happy. She wouldn't let me hold you. She clung to you and wouldn't put you in your crib even when you fell asleep. I was at university, and she never once asked how it was going. All she could talk about was you. I heard every detail of your birth. Your eating and sleeping schedule. Your bodily functions." Linda picks off a piece of lint and tosses it to the floor. "That was the last time we saw each other or talked. We just lost touch."

I put down my biscuit. "Did she talk to you about my da?"

"What do you mean?"

"Like, who was my da?"

"Heavens! It's Seamus. Why do you ask?"

"I just wondered if it might've been Paddy or someone else."

"Your mother thought Paddy was an eejit. Cocky. Self

160

absorbed. And he was. But he was also charming. Even I fell under his spell for a time." Linda brushes aside a wisp of her short hair that had fallen in her round face. "That drove Annie mad."

"Did he seem to like her?"

"He didn't think much of her. She'd follow me around. Sometimes I'd convince her to go out with us, but she'd sit back and sulk."

"I thought maybe she and Paddy, you know, got together."

Linda raises her finely tweezed eyebrows and shakes her head. "No, I'm pretty sure that never happened. When I left to go to university in London, I told Paddy and some others to keep an eye out for Annie and ask her to go out. Paddy said he would. The next thing I hear, she's married Seamus. My parents told me. Not Annie." She purses her lips. "That hurt. I called, and she told me about being with Seamus a couple of times and getting pregnant. It was...unexpected."

"Why's that?"

Linda sips her water. A breeze from an open window ruffles her hair.

I say, "Please. I really need to make sense of why she tried to kill herself."

Linda's eyes meet mine. She nods and says, "I didn't see her getting together with any of our mates. Your mother didn't trust people easily, especially men."

"Ma never said anything about her childhood," I say, realizing I'd never thought to ask her about it either.

"She didn't tell many people." Linda unwinds the scarf around her neck. "Let me tell you. Your grandmother's straight from Satan's womb." Her tone is harsh. I stare at her with my mouth open, unsure what to say. I've never heard my grandma described this way. "Oh, yes, she is. Have you seen your mother's feet?"

Ma always wore ratty brown slippers in the house and boots whenever she went outside. "No, now that I think of it, I haven't."

The melancholy sound from a cello drifts down the hall. A door squeaks shut, and only the muffled sound of the strings lingers.

"Well, I did once. They were completely scarred. When I asked Annie about them, she came up with some flimsy reason why they looked like that. But, eventually, she told me."

Linda reaches for a pack of cigarettes under a stack of papers and tries to extract one. It's empty. She tosses the wrapper toward the bin. It misses. The ashtray on the edge of her desk is full of butts. She picks up one that is half used and turns it over in her fingers.

"Your grandmother made her pick the switches. She told me that she had to pick the right branch. Not too short. Then remove the leaves. If she took too long picking it—or if she chose one that was too old and brittle—the beating lasted longer. It was for anything she felt Annie did wrong. Not cleaning the grout completely with the toothbrush and bleach. Eating her crisps too loudly." She lights the cigarette. "Annie said she used to scream, and your grandmother would stuff a dirty sock in her mouth." She inhales deeply and then blows the smoke through gritted teeth. "Lovely God-fearing woman, my arse."

"Did she tell Granda? Anyone?"

Linda shakes her head. "She really did have problems trusting people."

I mutter, "Mr. Walters knew that."

162

Linda stamps out the cigarette. "He tried to get me alone once, and I told him in no uncertain terms to stay the hell away from me. Told his wife, too. I warned Annie, but she said he was nice, and that I misunderstood him." Linda flips her head back and her face contorts. "Like hell I did."

"Did she tell you about a relationship with him?"

"Not in so many words, but I knew." She pushes the ashtray away and doesn't look at me. "She stopped talking to me about him. In a way—and I feel bad about this—I was relieved that she had someone else to talk to. She didn't hang on me as much."

"Do you think *he* could be my father?" I ask.

She turns toward me and shakes her head. "Seamus is your father. I never heard any differently. And he's a decent guy. A bit dull compared to Paddy, but kind and very loyal."

"What do you know about their relationship? Da and Paddy's?"

"What's to know? Mates for a long time. They played rugby. Inseparable, really. I have no idea if they are still friends or not. Are they?"

"Yes, quite."

Linda glances at her watch. "Eliza, I'm sorry, but my husband is waiting for me, so I have to go now." She straightens her skirt. "I wish I could have been more helpful."

My ankle's stiff when I get up and set my foot down. I limp somewhat as we walk down the hallway. When we reach the front door, a group of girls darts past us into the school. Linda returns their waves. After I mutter thanks for taking time to talk to me, Linda embraces me. Her silk scarf brushes my cheek. "Please tell Annie I say hello and would love to see her." As she releases me, she says, "Take care of her."

Chapter Twenty-Five

I can't believe that Grandma, who made my First Communion dress, abused Ma.

People pass by, engaged in conversation. Avoiding their faces, I look down, trying with every fiber of my body to hold it together as I walk the few streets to the car. My hands shake as I dig for my keys in the bottom of my bag. Inside the car, I pound the wheel and hunch over.

After I finally calm down, I call the hospital and ask for Ma. Again I'm told she refuses calls and visitors. I beg the clerk to let me talk to the doctor. After waiting for what seems an eternity, I'm told Dr. Kilkenny is unavailable. She will see me tomorrow morning at nine o'clock.

After three months of waiting, it's something.

A hotel nearby looks dodgy, but it's cheap and will do for tonight. I buy fish and chips wrapped in newspaper and retreat to my small room with peeling paint and stained carpet. I call Ryan. It goes straight into voicemail. Lying on the lumpy mattress, I pull up the thin blanket that reeks of cigarettes. Flipping through the channels on the clunky television, I think about Ma and her miserable childhood. About everything.

Eventually, I drift into a restless sleep.

The next morning I easily find St. Patrick's University Hospital on St. James Street. A prominent plaque recognizes Jonathan Swift as the founder more than 250 years ago. The receptionist directs me to Dr. Kilkenny's office. There, a woman with grey-sprinkled hair held back with a pair of slides, gets up and walks around her desk to greet me. Dressed in dark trousers and a tasteful sweater, she extends her hand. "Mary Kilkenny. It's nice to finally meet you. Your mother's a delightful woman."

I stand there awkwardly. "I never heard anyone describe her like that."

"How would you describe her?" Dr. Kilkenny points to a small, round table near the window and motions for me to sit down.

I sit on the edge of the high-backed chair. "I dunno. It's just, she never did anything. Just cooked and cleaned. Looked out the window." Dr. Kilkenny settles in the other chair, smoothes her sweater, and folds her hands on her lap. I look expectantly at her and say, "So is she better?"

"Improving. She especially likes the group sessions and interacting with some of the other residents."

I lean in. "When can I see her?"

Dr. Kilkenny's eyelids droop, hooding her wide-set eyes that are magnified under her thick, round glasses. "Dear, I know you made the long drive to see her. But she has chosen to separate from family while she tries to get well. I know that's hard to understand."

"But she let Da visit." My voice sounds whinier than I intend.

"Yes. She needed to talk to him about some things."

I stare at a vase full of flowers in the middle of the table. A few chrysanthemum petals have dropped onto the polished surface. I look out the window into a courtyard where people are clustered on benches beneath a grey sky. Swallowing hard, I say, "But *I* need to see her. There are things *I* need to talk to her about." I try hard not to, but I cry.

"Of course you do." Dr. Kilkenny reaches for a box of tissues, takes one out, and hands it to me. Her voice softens. "What I have to do, though, is make sure that it's the right thing for your mother." She touches my arm gently. "Dear, she's really making progress, and I don't want to set her back."

I wipe my eyes. "How could seeing *me* set her back?"

Dr. Kilkenny gathers the fallen petals from the table and holds them in her hand. "It's normal to feel anger and hurt. It's hard for your mother to face you because she didn't want to hurt you."

Outside, in the hall, a child starts wailing. I turn and look out the door into the hallway. A toddler has flung himself onto the floor. A man reaches down and picks up the flailing boy, catches my eye, and mouths, "Sorry." Dr. Kilkenny gets up and closes the door, which muffles the retreating cries. I grab another tissue and blow my nose. Dr. Kilkenny sits back down and pushes the tissue box closer.

The silence hangs like the morning fog. I look out the window into the garden. There's a small fountain. In addition to the patients sitting on the benches, there are couples walking along the path holding hands.

I look toward the wall with its cracked plaster and say, "I don't know what to do. I don't have a mother, a father, or a home anymore." I hold my head in my hands. "And I don't have any idea how to help her."

"You can help her by giving her the space she needs. And by taking care of yourself," the doctor says.

Choking back tears, I reach for my bag. It's caught on the leg of the chair. I tug, but it's stuck. Still, I yank on it. Dr. Kilkenny folds her hand around mine. She sighs. "Let me talk to her and see if we might arrange a short visit." She raises a finger. "But I'll be there to cut it short if I deem it necessary."

"Absolutely. Thank you." I scoot my chair back. Then I think of something. "Were you there when Da came?"

"For the first visit. Not the second."

"The second?"

"The next day. He bought her some new clothes and brought them by."

I sit back. "But he never shops. Except for fishing tackle."

"Your mother was pleased. And touched. I don't think she asked him to do it. Up until then, she wore the clothes we provided, which aren't very smart."

"I don't recall a time when he bought her a gift for her birthday or Christmas without my help."

"He did a fine job. After that, she started fixing her hair. Just combing and parting it differently, at first. Then she asked if she could get a haircut. Now she has an adorable style that suits her."

I can barely form a picture of Ma in my mind from before, let alone imagine what she might look like now. It dawns on me that I don't even have a picture of her.

"How long do you think she'll be here?"

"Your mother is actually staying at St. Edmundsbury, five miles from here, just outside the village of Lucan. There, she has her own room. When your mother's ready, we'll look for transitional lodging."

"What's that mean?"

"She's decided not to go back to Louisburgh. We're exploring options."

"I'll take care of her," I say.

Dr. Kilkenny shakes her head. "She doesn't need or want you taking care of her. That's one of the reasons that I'm not sure she's ready to see you. We're working on getting her strong enough to deal with the issues that contributed to her depression, and you have been her sole reason for living."

"Then why did she try to kill herself?"

"I'm not sure if this will make sense to you. On one level, your mother, by trying to take her own life, reclaimed it."

I gasp. "What?"

"It's hard to understand, I know, but she took control. She made the choice about living or dying."

"That's rubbish!"

"Your mother never felt she had power. Others made choices for her, or she felt compelled to make certain choices based upon circumstances. Your mother didn't see any future or have any hope when she came in. Now she's seeing that she does."

"But if she gets away from Louisburgh, it'll be better."

"She carries memories with her wherever she goes. Her thought process affects her moods and her behavior. She's making choices about where she's going to live, what she's going to do, and how she's going to interact with people in her life. She wants a relationship with you, but she needs to figure some things out for herself, as well."

"Like what?"

"There is the issue of earning money, as your mother didn't continue her education or have a trade. But she's proving to have a gift with pottery, and we're exploring options. We're taking it step by step."

"I'll get a job. A flat."

"You should take steps to take care of yourself." She pauses, eyes magnified by her thick lenses. "I can even recommend a therapist for you. It might be helpful in dealing with your own feelings."

My back straightens. "I'm quite fine, thank you." I stand. "I'm sorry I took so much of your time. Will you call me when I can visit her?"

"Absolutely. Please write down your number so I have it." Dr. Kilkenny slides a tablet over.

As I write my number, I say, "Whether she wants my help or not, I'm going to get to the bottom of things that *do* affect me." Then I hand Dr. Kilkenny my number, thank her, and walk out.

Chapter Twenty-Six

Low, grey clouds obscure the sun as I leave St. Patrick's Hospital. As I amble toward the car, a breeze blows my hair into my eyes. The air is crisp. Passing an Internet cafe, I catch a whiff of roasting coffee beans. It lures me inside. People of varying ages and ethnic backgrounds crowd the tables. I order cappuccino with an extra shot of espresso and wait until a computer becomes available.

The buzz of people and caffeine rejuvenates me as I search the Internet for possible jobs. I debate calling Maeve to check in on things at the B&B, but I know she'd bite my head off for implying that she might not have everything under control. Even Granda hasn't called me in weeks. Suddenly I recall that he was negotiating the purchase of a flat in Dublin that he intended to let out short-term. It dawns on me that it might be available if the deal closed before he went on holiday. I send him a quick email to check.

When my cell phone rings an hour later, I don't recognize the number, but I answer it anyway. A monotone voice informs me that she's the scheduler at DNA Specialists. "I was told to set up a time for you to review the results of the testing. Or we can put them in the post."

I say, "There's no place to mail them. I'll come by." I can barely hear her, so I step outside. "I thought it would take a week or so?"

"It can, but not always. There are several slots open tomorrow. We also had a cancelation for today at two o'clock, although that's short notice."

"I can come today," I tell her.

The testing center is located at the edge of the business district near the waterfront. Its red brick building has a crumbling façade. The building next door is for sale. As I walk toward the entrance, I smell rotting fish. Inside, the lobby is littered with discarded bottles and wrappers. The tenant list directs me to the fourth floor. The elevator is out of order, so I clomp up the stairs.

I'm breathless when I reach the fourth floor. The hall is lined with doors bearing the names of different tenants. At the end is a glass door marked "DNA Specialists." A bell rings when I push the door open. An unattended reception desk is feet from the door in the windowless office. Magazines cover a faux-wooden table that separates two wooden chairs. Within a few minutes a girl with spiky hair and pierced eyebrows arrives and says, "Can I help you?"

"I'm Eliza Conroy, and I have a two o'clock appointment."

"Oh, right." With a look of complete boredom, she checks my identification and leads me to an office just off the reception area.

A man in a wrinkled brown suit with his hair swept to

the side of his balding head rises and holds out his hand. "Patrick O'Neill. Please sit down." He motions to a chair and slips on black-rimmed reading glasses. "I was just reviewing the test results."

The chair wobbles as I sit and shift my weight to find a steady position. My ankle throbs from climbing the stairs. My breath is rapid and high in my chest. Leaning forward, I wait while traffic hums outside the closed window. In the other room, the receptionist cackles on the phone about a band she wants to see.

Mr. O'Neill furrows his brow as he ruffles through the paper. "Let's see..." On his desk, between towering stacks of files, are a half-eaten sandwich and a metal ashtray filled with butts. He keeps flipping through a file. At one point, he coughs and spits into a handkerchief.

I look back toward the receptionist. She's filing her nails and flipping through a magazine while talking on the phone. Outside the window, a pigeon alights on a ledge, then flies away. The receptionist squeals and then covers her mouth. She turns her back toward the wall. I can't hear the conversation now.

Finally, with a heavy sigh, Mr. O'Neill returns the paper to the file and closes it. "I've looked at the test results for Seamus Conroy, Paddy McDonald and William Walters." Pushing his reading glasses onto top of his head, he leans back in his chair. The air is stale. It reeks of perspiration. He looks at me with bloodshot eyes and says, "There's no match."

Chapter Twenty-Seven

Seagulls squawk and dive for food along the waterfront. It's been hours since I left with the news. Still, I keep walking.

I tell myself that I have to accept that I may never know who my father is. Da said Ma didn't remember anything when he found her in the pasture. Who knows what happened after Paddy left Ma there alone? Does it even matter now? I pull my jacket in tighter and stare at the boats in the harbor, the wide expanse of water, and the thick dark clouds.

As I walk, unsure where I'm going, I tell myself that I can't help Ma...that I have to accept that Ma may choose not to see me. Maybe not now. Maybe not ever.

A horn sounds, deep and low. A stiff breeze slaps my face. Dr. Kilkenny's words resurface in my mind: "Take care of yourself." I yank up my collar and turn back toward my car. From the car, I phone Granda. When he answers, I hear loud voices and traffic in the background. I tell him that I'm in Dublin and ask if the flat is available.

"It's open for the next three weeks, then it's let. Why?"

I say, "I came to see Ma. I need a place to crash." Clearly he hadn't opened my email.

"She okay?" Even with the background noise, I detect concern.

"Yeah. Getting better, they say."

"We'll try to call on her when we come through in a couple of weeks."

"She's not seeing visitors." My voice is steady and firm. "Even if she were, seeing Grandma might upset her."

"That right? Well, use the flat if you want. It's a mess. Closing got delayed, so things are behind schedule. We'll be back the week before it's let."

"I'll tidy up."

"Thanks, love. I'll call the caretaker so there'll be a key for you."

I write down the address and the chores Granda wants me to do while I'm there. After hanging up, I program my GPS and set out to find the place.

It turns out the flat is near Trinity College, in an upscale apartment building. The caretaker, alerted to my arrival, is just finishing dinner. He produces a key, shows me the assigned parking spot, and escorts me to the top floor. The spacious flat smells like fresh paint and new carpet. There's a patio with a nice view of manicured lawns. New furniture, complete with tags, is in place. Boxes, taped and marked, are stacked in every room. There's no food in the fridge, which is fine—I have no appetite.

Sitting on a couch facing sliding glass doors leading out to the patio, I rest my hand on the soft fabric and stare into the night sky. My eyes grow heavy, so I curl into a ball and fall asleep.

The next morning I have a kink in my neck and an imprint of the couch's textured pattern on my face. My stomach grumbles. Grabbing my coat and bag, I set out to explore the area. On St. George's Street I find a cafe and order a toasted breakfast sandwich and tea. People dart in on their way to work, or to class, or wherever. I finish half the sandwich and wrap the rest to take with me.

My ankle aches from so much walking the past few days, so I elevate it when I get back to the flat and search for jobs on the Internet. There's not much available that pays any sort of decent wage, but I make a list and plan to go out later.

Organizing the flat is a welcomed distraction. Granda said to start with Grandma's boxes, labeled according to rooms. In the kitchen, there's a bucket under the sink, rubber gloves, and household cleaner. I fill the bucket with soapy water, slip on the gloves, and wipe down all the cabinets and surfaces. Then I rip open the boxes marked "Kitchen" and put things away.

I move from room to room, getting things in order. Nothing I unpack looks familiar.

Eventually, there are only two small boxes left. Closed with masking tape, they are marked with Granda's perfect handwriting: "Business" on one. "Storage" on the other. I lift them. They feel like papers. Stacking the boxes, I carry them down the narrow hall to a small bedroom with a single bed, and a desk, and a window facing another apartment building.

Lifting the boxes overhead, I try to set them on the shelf inside the tiny closet. Despite my height, it's hard to reach; standing on tiptoe still hurts. I can only stretch my arms. As I try hoisting the boxes onto the shelf, they fall backwards toward my face. I grip the bottom box, but the other one slides onto the floor and smashes open.

Sitting on the floor among the spilled contents, I sweep the papers into a pile. I right the papers—mostly business letters and rental agreements for the cottages—and begin

175

filling the box. There are cancelled checks and insurance policies that I also stack inside.

When I have most of the contents back in the box, I scan the carpet for anything I've missed. Unlike the carpet elsewhere in the flat, this carpet is worn and stained. Against the wall, in the corner, is a letter-sized white envelope. I scoot over and grab it.

The envelope is unsealed. I lift the flap and pull out photographs.

The lighting in the top picture is dim. I can't tell if it's day or night. Ma is sitting on the bed. It's neatly made. Behind her, there's the same painting that hangs in all the upstairs bedrooms at the B&B: the Virgin Mary smiling down at the infant Jesus.

Ma looks like she did in the yearbook, with the same hair. Flat. Like her eyes.

I gasp.

Ma's blouse is unbuttoned to her navel, revealing her bra. Her thin lips are puckered unnaturally. Her eyes stare ahead, like those of a trapped animal.

My breath locks inside my chest. Taken on a Polaroid camera, the picture sticks to my hand. Numbly, I turn to the next one.

It's the same room. The bedside table lamp is on. The duvet is folded back. Neat. Tidy. Ma's face is turned away. Her eyes are closed. She is lying bare-chested on the bed with her hands behind her back.

My cell phone rings in the next room. I sink down onto the carpet. It smells like cat urine. My stomach knots. The walls, the color of dirty water, have holes where pictures once hung. I lean against the wall, holding the photographs and staring out the window at the neighboring brick building. Everything blurs. The phone stops ringing. The only sound is my own shallow breathing.

I force myself to look at the next photograph. The lampshade is askew. The pillows and bedding lie on the floor. Alone on the bed is Ma. She's naked. Her face is as contorted as her body. Her eyes are wide but empty.

A vile taste rises in my mouth. I try choking it back, but can't. The vomit spews across the floor. Hunched over, I heave until there's nothing left. Then, clutching the pictures, I scramble to my feet and stagger out the room. Tears stream down my face.

I pace the flat. Then, needing air, I go out onto the patio. The cool evening air blows my hair back. Closing my eyes, I see Ma's eyes but hear Granda's voice telling me what to do to put everything in its place. I recall, as a child, sitting on his lap and digging in his front shirt pocket for the hard candies. I recall the feel of his strong arms hugging me. And I shudder.

Still gripping the pictures, I carry them to the main bedroom and place them carefully into my suitcase along with the rest of my things. Then I leave the key on the table, pick up my suitcase that I had brought in and slam the door behind me.

Chapter Twenty-Eight

I hear myself slurring my words as I order yet another pint of ale. Music blares and patrons crowd into the small, smoke-filled pub. Sitting on a stool at the bar, I grip my empty glass and wait for the refill while I stare at a mounted, mute television screen. The news is on. When the barman slides the pint in front of me, I turn away. I recognize the look all too well. This is the third day in a row that I've found my home here, returning at night to the dodgy place where I first stayed in Dublin.

My jaw is clenched, and my back hunched. I can't get the pictures of Ma out of my head. It's her eyes, the eyes I never noticed when they were in front of me, that haunt me now.

I keep checking my phone to see if Ryan has returned my call from this morning when, after two days, I finally dragged myself out of bed to search for a job. I want to report that I'm fine, even though I'm not. But he hasn't called me back. Not yet.

I rotate my glass and watch the amber fluid swirl close to the rim.

Will I tell him the truth? Will I tell *anyone* the truth? Will the weight of the truth crush me like it did Ma?

An overfed man with thinning hair squeezes in between

me and the person on the stool next to me. "Howya." He bumps my arm as I lift the glass to my mouth. It spills all over my shirt.

"Shite." I wipe my face with the back of my hand and grab for a napkin.

"Sorry, miss. Let me make it up to you." He winks and motions for the barman to bring me another. "How's it going?"

"Been better."

"Aw, a fine thing here alone." He puts his arm around my shoulder. The ripe smell of the docks and of tobacco permeate his overcoat.

"Hump off."

"Why such the puss face?" He leans in closer. Whiskey rides his breath. When I turn away and focus my attention on the mute television, he brushes his hand across my breast and says, "Lovely."

I throw the rest of my ale in his face. "Keep your hands off me, you prick."

He staggers back. "What the…?"

I glare at him, daring him to say or do anything. My body coils, ready to spring. People around us turn and stare. He scowls, cusses under his breath, and stomps off. I grip my empty glass and close my eyes.

The barman slides another pint in front of me and mutters, "On the house." He pushes a bowl of nuts closer and then looks at the television screen. A reporter is interviewing an attractive woman in a smart business suit. I can't hear the interview, but sprawled across the bottom of the screen are the words: Clara McShane sues Catholic Church. Ms. McShane is smiling and waving a document. In the background, people are cheering. The barman finishes wiping

179

down the bar and slings the towel over his shoulder. He says, "I'll be damned."

⟋⟍

By the end of the week I get a job answering phones for a software development company. I make just enough to afford a flat in the dodgy part of town. When Ryan and I finally connect, I tell him things are grand. He suggests coming for a visit, but I tell him I'm too busy with the new job and with getting settled. I tell him I haven't yet heard about the DNA results.

There's a lot I don't tell him about: Da and Paddy. Grandma. Granda.

Each day I read or hear about the clerical sexual abuse scandal and Clara McShane, the attorney who exposed it.

Could I expose Granda, the most respected man in Louisburgh? Who would believe me and Ma? Would Ma even want me to tell anyone after she hid what happened and then buried it all these years?

What good would telling do?

I know the harm it would do. It would destroy Granda and Grandma, who love me and who have done so much for me...for the community...for the Church.

Yet they treated Ma worse than a dog. They destroyed her. They destroyed our family.

The anger boils inside me. I can't sleep or eat. When I look in the mirror, I see dark circles beneath my eyes. Each time I see Granda's number come up on my phone, I feel like screaming.

The truth imprisons me.

I toss my cell phone in the rubbish bin and buy a new phone with a new number. Then I call Clara McShane's office. Just to see.

~

Two days later, I arrive at the four story professional building near Ballsbridge, take the elevator to the fourth floor, and push through two enormous mahogany doors with gold lettering: Clara McShane, Solicitor.

A perky receptionist greets me. When I introduce myself, she smiles. "Please have a seat. Ms. McShane is finishing a matter and will be out shortly. May I get you something to drink while you wait?"

I say, "No, thank you." I sit in a zebra-striped chair, pick up a magazine from the glass table, and glance at the modern artwork on the walls.

Within ten minutes, a petite woman with big, highlighted hair appears and shakes my hand. Wearing a cream-colored suit and heels, she looks close to forty. "You must be Eliza. I'm Clara McShane. Very nice to meet you. Please come with me to my office. Did Nikki offer you something to drink?"

"Yes, I'm fine," I say as I limp slightly on the way to her office. It's the first day I've tried walking without the boot. I cringe.

"Bum leg?"

"I broke my ankle running. It's getting better."

When we reach her office, she motions toward a white couch in a sitting area. The office is immense. From the chair opposite the couch, Clara McShane smiles at me, arching painted-on eyebrows. "What can I do to help you?"

"I don't really know where to begin."

"Start at the beginning, love."

As I spill everything, Clara doesn't interrupt. At times she closes her eyes and shakes her head. She jots a few notes. When I finish, she says, "Your poor mother. You, too. This is a lot to deal with at your age. I commend you for doing what you have already."

"Do you think you can help?"

"I need to look at everything, including the pictures, and check some things out with my colleagues. You say you found some hairs in a bag inside your baby book, and don't know whose they are. Or, if they are your grandfather's?"

I nod.

"Testing them, even if the root of the hair is there, may not help us, but I'll check." She jots a note. "What your mother has gone through is unconscionable. While it's too late for criminal charges, we can purse civil damages. Money can't change what happened, but it can help take care of your mother now."

"I just got a job. It doesn't pay much, but…"

"I charge a contingent fee based upon what he pays. You don't pay me."

I relax. "Oh."

"Once you sign the agreement, I'll be able to represent you. Then I'll need your grandfather's telephone number, along with the pictures and the hair sample. We'll meet again after I've done the preliminary research."

I write Granda's number down and promise to bring everything else by tomorrow on my way to work.

"Lovely. Also, I want you present at the meeting that I'm going to arrange with him."

I hadn't thought about that. How could I face him?

Clara leans forward and grasps my hands. "You need to trust *me*. Do you?" She stares intently at me, jaw set, and I nod and try sitting taller.

~~~~~~~~

After two long weeks, the meeting date arrives. I can only imagine how often Granda has tried to call me. Only Ryan, Clara McShane, and Dr. Kilkenny have my new number. My sweaty palms grip the water glass as I sit in Clara's office waiting for the meeting to begin. She felt it best that I wait in her office until Granda and his solicitor are in the conference room.

I strain to hear whether Granda has arrived and keep glancing at the crystal clock on the corner of the credenza. Only ten more minutes to wait.

When I hear Granda's voice drift down the hall, I focus on taking deep breaths. A sip of water cools my throat, but not the burning in my stomach.

I hear Clara directing Granda and his solicitor to the conference room. Then, her heels click down the hardwood floors, and she appears in the doorway. "Show time. Remember what we talked about. I'll do the talking. Don't say anything unless I tell you to, okay? I'll go in first. You follow just a minute or so after me. Okay?" I nod and try swallowing to loosen the lump lodged in my throat. She touches my arm. "You *will* be fine."

I square my shoulders and follow Clara in the wake of her perfume, the scent of musky roses. My ankle twinges in my new flats, but I walk with only a slight limp.

As Clara opens the conference room door, she says, "Thank you for waiting, gentlemen. My client has arrived." She steps aside. I walk through the door. Sun streams through the floor-to-ceiling windows. Granda turns, and we stand face to face.

Chapter Twenty-Nine

Granda stands before me, dressed in a starched white shirt and navy pinstriped suit, and bearing a Mediterranean tan from his holiday in Italy. I feel like my legs are going to buckle. His jaw drops. "Eliza! What are you doing here?"

Clara grabs my elbow and ushers me to the chair next to her at the rectangular conference table. A coffee carafe and Belleek china cups and saucers sit in the center on a silver tray with cream and sugar.

Granda takes a step forward, furrowing his thick brow. His voice booms. "What's this about?"

Clara says in a firm tone, "Business."

"What does Eliza have to do with business?" Granda's eyes dart between me and Clara. They lack all the softness I knew as a child. "You said there was a proposition you had been asked to present on behalf of an important client."

"This *is* my important client," Clara says. She sits down and waits for Granda and his stout solicitor to do the same. Her eyes never leave his.

"Are you going to tell us what this is about, *Miss* McShane?" Granda's grey-haired solicitor demands.

"Why yes, I will, *Andrew*." Clara splays her manicured nails on top of a file. "Let me begin by stating that I do appreciate your coming in for this meeting, Mr. O'Donnell—or may I call you Edward?"

"You can call my client, *Mr. O'Donnell*."

"Absolutely, Andrew. *Mr. O'Donnell*, my client has engaged me to present a business proposition for your consideration. We fully expect that you will consent to the terms, so let me lay them out for you." She glares at the two men. "S*it down*." Granda and his solicitor exchange glances and sit.

Clara says, "First, my client would like you to sign over the titles to the cottages she manages for you, including the one she lives in, to her mother, Annie Conroy."

"What? Are you crazy? Why would I do that? Have you gone mental, Eliza?" Granda narrows his eyes and snarls, "Where is this coming from? Who has put you up to this?"

My gut contracts, and I look down. Clara warned me not to speak.

"Second," Clara continues, "My client would like you to sign over the title to the home in Naples, Italy, as well to Annie Conroy."

"You've got to be kidding! Why the hell would I do that?" yells Granda.

Clara holds Granda's gaze. "My client fully recognizes that you may wish to continue to occupy the residence in Naples, and she's agreeable to your paying rent to her mother based upon the prevailing rates, to be reviewed on the first of each calendar year. Should you decline the rate presented, you and your wife will have thirty days to vacate the home."

"This meeting is over." Granda's solicitor stands and Granda starts to get up, too.

"I don't think you want to leave until you hear all the terms," Clara says.

They scowl and fold their arms over their chests. Granda shakes his head disdainfully. This time, I don't look away. He runs his hand through thick red, grey-tinged hair and glances at his solicitor who nods slightly. Finally, they sit.

"As I was saying, those are the first two terms. The next terms involve money being paid to Annie, Eliza and Seamus Conroy. Each of them. Separately. The sums are clearly outlined. Finally, you will assume all legal fees." Clara pulls documents from the file folder and slides them in front of Granda.

The solicitor snatches the documents and begins reviewing them. "This is ridiculous! Why in God's name would my client even consider entertaining these propositions?"

"Well, there are several very good reasons that Edward, I mean *Mr. O'Donnell*, would seriously consider and sign the documents." Clara pulls out the envelope, then the photographs. She spends considerable time looking at each one. As she does, her expression grows graver. Then she hands the stack of photographs to Granda's solicitor.

I can barely breathe. I watch Granda for a reaction. His mouth twitches slightly. Nothing more.

His solicitor says, "What the hell is this about? Do you care to share?"

"Oh, pardon me. I forgot that perhaps your esteemed client may not have shared all aspects of his life with his trusted advisor." Clara slides the photographs over. "Would anyone care for something else to drink?" When no one responds, she pours me a cup of black coffee.

The sound of Clara drumming her nails on the polished conference table echoes through the room as Granda's solicitor looks at the pictures and lets out a soft gasp. My hand shakes as I lift a cup of coffee to my lips. I almost gag on the bitter brew, but swallow it. The china clinks as I lower my cup onto the saucer.

Granda's broad shoulders droop as a deep breath escapes his pursed lips. He closes his eyes.

His solicitor says, "I suppose you're going to tell me what these photographs have to do with my client?"

I hold my breath and watch Clara lean forward. Her hair and makeup are as perfect as her posture. "Edward, would you like to explain, or shall I?"

Granda shifts in the chair and looks out the window at the cloudless sky.

In a raised tone, Clara says, "Your client sexually assaulted his own daughter and fathered my client." She gathers the pictures and returns them to her file. "Is this now clear?"

Granda's solicitor says, "You can't prove that!"

"Is it possible you haven't heard about me? Didn't you do your research? I expose secrets. The worst kind. The Church's. Now yours." She narrows her eyes. "You would do well to *not* underestimate me."

Granda's cheeks redden as Clara speaks. He refuses to look at her. Or at me.

Clara reaches back into the file. "DNA testing is a marvelous thing." She pulls out a plastic bag and turns it over in her thin fingers. "Especially when your client leaves his own pubic hair." As I take another sip of coffee, she takes out a sheet of paper and holds it up with the text facing her. "Would you care to read the results?"

Granda buries his head in his large hands. A low, guttural sound rises from his chest.

Clara ignores him. "You might be interested to know that I did my own research on your client, Andrew. I wonder if the fine people of Louisburgh know that he is related to one of the most powerful families in Ireland, albeit not as closely as he'd like, I'm sure. You might even say they're quite distant relations, but, I'm guessing, equally touchy about their reputation. Or perhaps I'm wrong?" She lowers her voice to a purr. "It seems there are many sides to Edward."

Granda's solicitor tugs at his tie, then folds his stubby fingers, and casts a sideways look at Granda.

Clara gathers her files and stands. "We are going to leave you two alone to discuss our terms. I will return in five minutes with a notary to ask for Edward's signature on the documents." She touches my arm and I follow her out.

Together we walk, our steps in sync until we reach her office. There, I burst out crying. Clara hugs me. "You did beautifully. I know how hard that was. Go ahead and cry. It's almost over. You will never have to see him again. I have prepared a document that states that he is not to have any unsolicited contact with you, your mother, or Seamus going forth. If he does attempt to contact any of you, he'll pay for each such contact."

Between sobs, I ask, "Do you really think he'll sign them?"

"Yes, I do. Did you see his face when I mentioned the DNA testing?"

Shivers creep up my spine. "I don't think I can face him again."

"You won't have to. It's time to sign the documents. I'll take care of that. Even if he wants to speak to you, I'll decline the request. You stay here. I predict we'll be done shortly." Clara pats my hand and marches from the room like a warrior to battle. Even without conclusive DNA testing, she won. They never called her bluff.

I collapse on the couch, shaking. It took every ounce of energy I had not to cry or scream vile things at Granda. My mother's rapist. My father. Tears soak the pillow I've clutched to my face.

Within fifteen minutes, I hear the elevator ding and Clara clip down the hall. She's wearing a wide grin as she plops in the chair across from the couch. "He signed each one and wrote the checks. Damn, I should have asked for more. Well, your mother doesn't have to worry about money now. She's free to move on and try to rebuild her life as best as she's able."

I put the pillow down and wipe my eyes. "Did he ask about Ma?"

Clara shakes her head and adjusts her jacket. "No. He didn't."

"I still wish we could make him really pay. And I'm not just talking money."

"You've exposed the truth. There's nothing he can do to undo or repair the damage, but he can make reparations. Each time he has to write a rent check to your mother, he will remember what he did." A smile spreads over her face. "I expect that'll kill him." Clara explains the process for transferring title and other matters that I need to discuss with Ma when she agrees to see me. If she does.

"What do I do now?"

"You and your mother have a chance to make your lives what you want. Figure out what you want to do and who you want to become. Travel. Go to university. Hell, even become a solicitor."

Nikki comes in announcing the next appointment. We rise and move toward the elevator. Clara stops me and goes to her desk. "I almost forgot. Here's the other thing we discussed." She hands me a sealed envelope. "Let me know if you need any assistance in this regard." She hugs me and releases me to an unknown future.

As I leave the building, I dig out my sunglasses, tuck the envelope into my bag, and hold my head high. It's time to return to Louisburgh to finish what I need to do.

Chapter Thirty

Driving on twisting roads through green pastures, I think of Ma's past that is my heritage: violence, pain, and lies. I think of my choices and what needs to be said and done before I'm free to live my life.

When I arrive in Louisburgh, I drive to Mr. Walters's house. The late afternoon sun beats on a weed patch in the small yard along the path to Mr. Walters's door. I knock. There's no answer and no dog barking. Next to the door, with a flat tire, is the three-wheeled Schwinn with the basket on the back. Peeking in the side window, I see dishes piled in the sink and a newspaper lying open on the table next to a teacup and saucer.

I drive back to the town square. Mr. Walters can't be far.

Cars line the streets while dogs roam looking for scraps or a rub behind the ears. I wonder if Maeve is keeping busy at the B&B and consider stopping by. Then I see Mr. Walters hobble out of the chemist carrying a small white prescription bag, with Johnny unleashed and trotting by his side.

Turning the car around, I drive back to Mr. Walters's house to wait. When he arrives, I step out and take off my sunglasses. "I was hoping to find you home."

"Well, I dare say, Eliza, I thought you would wander far

from home." Mr. Walters walks up the path, through the gate. "Yet you return."

"Sometimes we come home because there are things unsaid or undone."

"I just received a letter from that DNA place, but haven't opened it yet. Are you here to tell me the news?"

I say, "You're not my father."

He walks toward the door. "Now we know."

"There's a matter we need to discuss," I continue.

Mr. Walters turns the doorknob, then stops and looks at me. "What could that be?"

"Your resignation."

"I have no intention of resigning." He opens the door.

Before he can go inside, I say, "Either you resign or I'll expose all the relationships you've had with your students, not just Ma." I dig in my bag and produce an envelope. "I have a letter written by you to the headmaster announcing your immediate resignation. If you choose not to sign the letter, then I have one from my solicitor which I will bring to the headmaster notifying him of your transgressions over the years and including, as evidence, the many letters from Ma that I found in your house." My voice is strong. I narrow my eyes and cross my arms. "And from other girls. It's a fine package of letters you've kept over the years. What are they? Trophies?"

Mr. Walters bares his yellowed teeth. "Where did you get those?"

"You left them in the drawer near the bed. I found them when I stayed here after my surgery."

Johnny whines and looks up at Mr. Walters. With flaring nostrils, Mr. Walters swipes his hand at the dog's nose. "Shut up."

"This is what I can't figure out. Why did you leave them in the drawer in the room you put me in? Did you *want* me to find them?"

"It was a long time ago. I didn't remember they were there. And they're nothing." He avoids my eyes. "Many students become infatuated with their teachers."

"You exploited their trust. Their secrets." I hold out the envelope, this time closer to Mr. Walters's face.

"You don't have it in you." He steps forward.

I block him from going inside. "You'll resign. Or I'll tell."

Mr. Walters snarls, "What makes you think the headmaster, or others, will believe a girl traumatized by her mother's attempted suicide?"

"Are you going to sign this or not? If you don't, the headmaster will receive a letter from my solicitor."

Mr. Walters glares at me. I refuse to look away. Finally, Mr. Walters snatches the envelope. He opens it and reads the letter for his signature. I dig out a pen and hold it up. Without meeting my eyes, he grabs it. Using the door as a hard surface, he scribbles his name. Then, he flings the letter at me. I catch it before it falls into the dirt. He walks inside with Johnny and slams the door shut.

I stare at his signature before returning the letter to the envelope. Holding my head high, I get into the car and drive to the school, just a few streets away.

As it's the beginning of summer break, the school is unlocked but quiet inside. A light is on in the main office. Mrs. McCune's half full mug of tea sits next to the computer with its screensaver scrolling past. I call her name, but there's no answer. Along the back wall is a copy machine. It's turned on. Taking out the letter, I place it on the glass and make a copy and put it in my bag. Then I slip the original letter back into the envelope and seal it. Just off the main office is the headmaster's office. It's dark inside, but the door's ajar. I put the sealed envelope on his desktop and then walk out of the school without seeing anyone.

Inside my car, I open all the windows. The air whirls through the car as I drive to our cottage.

When I arrive, Da's car is parked in my spot. Without knocking, I push open the door and step over Da's muddy boots. His jacket is flung on the back of a chair. From the kitchen comes Da's rich, but off-key, baritone voice. Without calling out, I walk toward the kitchen. Unwashed dishes fill the sink. He's at the stove stirring something that smells like it is burning. There's an opened can of beans and a box of instant potatoes on the counter.

I clear my throat. Da's hand bumps the handle of the pan. It crashes to the floor and beans scatter on the floor. He wipes his hands on his pants and steps over the mess. "Eliza." He hugs me tightly. "I didn't think you'd come back."

Da's cheek is rough and his grip is tight. I close my eyes and inhale his scent. Then, I pull back. "Sorry to startle you. I need to talk to you." I walk into the living room.

He tucks his shirt into his wrinkled pants and follows me. The drapes are partly opened. His tackle box is open on the coffee table.

"It's about the test." I sit on the lumpy couch.

Da's face falls as he sits on the chair opposite me. He says, "I don't give a damn about the bloody test. We burned the envelopes. Didn't even open them." There are ashes in the fireplace. The peat bin is empty.

"Right. Well, I wanted a proper goodbye." My finger

brushes over the faded, worn fabric of the couch and rests on one of the burn spots from Da's cigars. I say, "And to tell you that I'm okay with Paddy. With the two of you."

Da's eyes mist. "It'd be easier without the bloke." He rubs the grey stubble on his chin.

"There are other places where it'd be easier being together."

Da shakes his head and wipes his eyes with his sleeve. In a low voice, he says, "We can't leave Louisburgh. It's our home."

I look at the pictures on the mantel. Each one is still in its place. I rise. "I've got to get back to Dublin. I've got a job there now."

"That right?"

"And a new phone number." I dig out a scrap of paper from my bag and write it down. I leave the number on the end table next to the ash tray.

Da hoists himself up and follows me toward the door. He picks up a shoebox from the side table. It's covered with a layer of dust. "Your ma called a few days ago and asked me to send her some photographs. I was going to mail them, but maybe you can give her the box?" He lifts the lid, picks up one and grins. "Aye, you were a cute wee one."

It's a picture of the three of us sitting around the kitchen table. There's a layer cake with white icing and two candles. A bright yellow bow holds back my straight red hair and I'm wearing a puffy flowered dress. Ma's face is close to mine, and Da is standing behind her. We are all smiling.

It dawns on me that Paddy took the picture. Our invisible but ever-present extra family member.

"Why don't you keep it? I'm sure there are others for her. And for me."

Da sighs. "Your ma's probably not coming back."

196

I say gently, "No. I don't think so."

Concern is etched into the lines of his face. "But how will she manage?"

"She will. I'll see to it." I take the box and grab my bag. "Granda has decided to give the title to the cottages—all of them—to her. You can manage them for Ma." I dig into my bag and hand Da a check. "This is from Granda. For you."

Da stares at the check. "What the bloody hell?"

"He wants to help Ma and you."

Da squints and cocks his head. "Doesn't seem like something he'd do."

"I hired a solicitor. She was brilliant and convinced Granda it was right to help take care of Ma. And, repay you too."

"*You* hired a solicitor? Shite, he'll never let me hear the end of it."

"If he bothers you in any way, let me know."

Da shakes his head while fingering the check. "I don't understand."

"In this case, you don't need to." After taking one more look around the cottage, I grab the shoebox and my bag. "I have to go."

I open the door. The flower box remains empty, but the smell of the sea floats in on the breeze and the sun sneaks behind a cloud.

Da says, "You'll come back to see me, won't you?"

I nod. He grips me in his massive arms and holds me tight. In a choked breath, I say, "Love you, Da."

Chapter Thirty-One

Nearly four months have passed since Ma's attempted suicide, and a month since my legal confrontation with Granda. I'm at work when I notice that I have a message on my cell phone. It's from Dr. Kilkenny. She asked me to call back. During my lunch break, I call Dr. Kilkenny. She tells me that Ma is moving to transitional housing soon and that she wants to see me. My shoulders relax and I feel lighter in response to the news.

"I can come any time." I glance at my watch. "Today?"

"No. Tomorrow around ten o'clock. After group. Remember, she's at St. Edmundsbury." Dr. Kilkenny provides me the address, and I find my supervisor to ask for the day off.

I can think of nothing else. How do I tell Ma all that I know? Would it make a difference? Should Ma be able to choose the secrets she wants to keep? But, how can I keep them after learning the truth? Could we ever have any relationship among the lies?

The next morning, I arrive early, carrying the shoebox of family photographs from Da. As I wait to see Ma, I meander through the circular path outside the main building on St. Edmundsbury's expansive grounds. There is a light mist. I keep checking the time on my phone. Finally, it's time to go inside. Dr. Kilkenny greets me in the reception area. "Your mother wants to meet you alone, without me there. In morning session today, the group encouraged her to do that. I respect her decision, and I think she's ready."

As we walk down the hallway, I get a glimpse inside a room where several women are working on a large loom. They look up as we pass. Further down the hallway, we stop outside a closed door. Hanging on the wall beside the door is a hand-painted ceramic sign: Annie's Room.

Dr. Kilkenny faces me. Touching my arm, she smiles kindly. "I'll be in my office at the end of the hall, just around the corner, if either of you needs me. The door will be open."

I watch her clip down the hall and turn. I knock softly. The shoebox of family photographs is tucked under my arm. I play with a strand of hair that's out of place. It's quiet except for the hum of the fluorescent light in the hall. I look up and notice the discolored ceiling tiles. Then there's movement in the room. I take a deep breath.

Ma opens the door. Her straight black hair, once unshaped and limp, is short and stylish. She's wearing a patterned blouse tucked into fitted jeans that highlight her trim, petite figure. "Eliza!" She steps forward and hugs me. Her arms feel strong.

As I bend down, returning her hug, I whisper, "I missed you." She pulls me closer, but doesn't say anything as she sways slightly, stroking my hair. She doesn't smell like I remember. It's lavender, not bleach or the perfume I give her every year.

Then Ma pulls back, grinning at me. There's a glimmer of gloss on her lips. She takes my hand and leads me to the neatly made double bed that takes up most of the room. We sit. Beside the bed, on a nightstand, there are self-help books stacked according to size with their spines lined up. After squeezing my hand, she lets go and folds her hands in her lap.

Muted voices pass by the door and then disappear. A window opposite the doorway takes up almost the entire wall. Even though it's mid-morning and the room is filled with natural light, the lamp near the bed is turned on. A small bronze medallion is on the table next to a book entitled *Daily Meditations*. I want to ask about the medallion, but I don't. Instead, I reach over and put my hand on the shoebox. "Da asked me to bring these photos."

"Thank you." She opens the lid and starts looking through them. I notice a touch of mascara and a soft shadow dusting Ma's lids. She smiles. "He didn't need to send so many."

"He kept some." I recall the picture of the three of us on my second birthday and the ones on the mantel. I look down at my hands. My fingernails are chewed to their nubs. A new, bad habit. I tuck my hands under my bottom.

Ma sorts through the pictures in silence. The ones of her and Da, she puts back into the box; the ones of me, she continues to hold. She lingers over a photo of me at my baptism, dressed in the christening gown that had been hers, as well. Ma's thin fingers rest on her parted lips. "You were just a baby," she whispers.

"Yeah." I don't know what else to say.

Ma replaces the pictures and closes the shoebox. She wipes the dust off the lid with her hand.

We sit side by side on the bed, just breathing. A tree branch sways outside the window, almost hitting the glass, but then it doesn't. The sky is overcast.

I want to ask questions but am too afraid of saying the wrong thing, so I wait.

Finally, Ma says, "So, how'd the race go? The one you were training for."

"It didn't," I tell her. "I went running on Croagh Patrick and I fell. It was stupid. I lost my footing when it started raining and broke my ankle and had to have surgery."

"Oh, Lord, no!" she gasps.

"Yeah, I was disappointed. It's getting better. Still sore, though. Luckily, I get to sit down at my job."

"Job?" Ma asks.

"Here in Dublin. Mostly I answer phones. It's dull, but it pays for my flat," I touch her arm. "You could come and see the flat. Maybe stay."

"A job here? And a flat?" Ma furrows her brow and pulls back her arm. "*Why?*"

My chest deflates. "So I can help you."

Ma looks around the room. "But Dr. Kilkenny has a place arranged for me."

"I can talk to Dr. Kilkenny. We could find a bigger place. Wouldn't you like that better?"

Ma's smile is unconvincing.

In the hallway, men are bantering about a contested rugby match. As their voices trail off, Ma turns to me. "I didn't ask you. How's Mikey?"

"Oh, hell. I haven't seen that bloke for a long time."

"Really? Is there someone else?"

I pause. "Nothing serious."

"Anyone I know?" she asks.

"Sometimes I hang out with Doc's son, Ryan. The vet. He lives in Westport."

Ma looks puzzled.

I say, "He helped you." I smooth out a wrinkle on the duvet. It's pilled and rough to my touch. "That day. Before the ambulance came. He helped stop the bleeding."

201

"Oh." Ma looks down. "I don't remember much."

I wait, thinking Ma might want to talk about it, but she looks away and says nothing.

Pulling my legs up onto the bed, I rub my ankle. "Ryan's turned out to be a good friend. Even though he's bossy and full of himself at times." I force a laugh. "He was helping me train for the race and talked me into running Croagh Patrick. We should have gotten down sooner to avoid the rain. But it came up pretty quickly."

Ma's expression is serious. "Do you like him? I mean, as more than friends?"

My gut twinges. I shrug. "He's been great. Really supportive." I can't help smiling. "And he's cute and sweet."

"But he's in Westport and you're here in Dublin?"

"That is one of the problems." My shoulders droop. "I don't know what I want. I just know I don't want to go back there. I can't." I start chewing on a fingernail, then stop. "There are loads of things I haven't sorted out yet."

"Like what?" Ma asks.

"Just stuff." I shift on the bed and look down at my gnawed cuticles. "But I will."

To change the subject, I ask about the activities at St. Edmundsbury. We chat about Ma's new interest in pottery, and she points out two fat, round pots perched on top of a rectangular cabinet. They are quite lovely. Above the bed, a ceramic crucifix hangs from a nail. Ma says she made it. Tucked behind it is a dried palm frond, the kind they give in church on Palm Sunday.

Ma answers my questions, but volunteers nothing. Several times she glances at the digital clock on the nightstand.

Ma takes a deep breath. Without meeting my eyes, she

says, "I'm so sorry you had to find me like that." Ma's shoulders sink and she starts sobbing. "What kind of mother does that?"

My gut contracts. I can't hold the tears back any longer. In between gulps of air, I say, "I didn't think you'd make it." I sob. Ma pulls me tighter and strokes my hair. Her breath is warm on my neck. I say, "I didn't think you'd ever want to see me again."

Hugging. Rocking. Crying. We do this for a long time. Then Ma pulls back, and we both wipe our eyes.

Ma says, "I couldn't face you. I'm ashamed that at the time I didn't care what my death might do to you. Or to your da." She looks out the window at the shrouded sun. "I only wanted to die, to be free. Not from you, love, but...it felt easier."

"You're better now, though, right?" I say.

"Getting there."

"Does that mean you can leave? With me?"

Brushing her hand across my damp cheek, she smiles weakly and says, "Love, I don't think that's best. For either of us."

"I can take care of you." My voice gets soft. "I need you. I need to know you're okay."

Ma tilts my head up. "You need to live your life."

"I *am*," I say. "I've got a job now, and my own place. I'm not going back to Louisburgh. Ever."

"Who's helping with the B&B?" Ma asks.

"Maeve's there. No doubt doing a better job."

"Still..."

"Granda understands that I need to leave Louisburgh. And that I need to help you." I lean my head against Ma's bony shoulder.

"It's good you're away." Ma looks down and wrings her

hands. "Good you don't have to rely on your granda for a job. For money."

The tree branch outside slaps against the windowpane, startling us both. The room is stuffy. It's hard to breath. The secrets and the loneliness are swallowing me up.

Finally, I can't hold back. "Ma, I know things now. That you couldn't tell me." Air swells in my chest and I say, "About Granda."

"What?" She bolts off the bed and begins pacing the room.

"Ma, please sit down. Let me explain." I go and wrap my arms around her. She tries to free herself, but I tighten my grip. "Just listen. It's going to be okay."

Ma breaks free and flees to the window.

"Please. I didn't want to upset you. Maybe I should get Dr. Kilkenny." There's light filtering in under the door and footsteps in the hall, but no voices.

She refuses to look at me. In a small voice, she says, "I'm fine."

I take a tentative step forward. Ma sneaks a look at me, but turns back toward the window. I pause. Her chest rapidly rises and falls. I step closer and, in a voice barely louder than a whisper, I say, "I know Granda's my father."

Ma gasps and turns to face me.

Quickly I add, "But when I found out, I hired a solicitor." I hold my hands out. "Everything's okay."

She sputters, "You hired a solicitor?"

I talk fast, "It's hard to explain, but pieces came together. I didn't see it at first. Nothing made sense. You left your ring. I found your journal." Ma grips her head, intertwining her hands in her fine hair. Moving closer, I whisper, "And, I found the pictures. The ones Granda took."

Ma starts crying hysterically. I put my hands on her shoulders. "Ma, I'm sorry." I try getting her to the chair. It's like corralling a wild animal. "We don't have to talk about this now." She finally sits, but won't look at me. I kneel in front of her and say, "I just didn't want secrets between us anymore." Ma covers her eyes, doubles over and makes low guttural noises. I try to hug her, but she pushes me away.

The look in her eyes scares me. I dash out of the room to find Dr. Kilkenny.

Chapter Thirty-Two

Dr. Kilkenny barks at me to get out of Ma's room, but I stand rooted in the doorway. Ma's sobbing in the chair while Dr. Kilkenny mutters words I can't hear. Ma's eyes had sparkled when I arrived that morning. Now they look like they did when I found her in the tub: hollow; vacant. Dr. Kilkenny comes over and pushes me out the door, telling me to wait in the family lounge. She slams the door shut.

I wander down the hall, past the receptionist and into the family lounge. Collapsing into a chair, I wait.

As soft instrumental music plays in the background, my mind replays every minute with Ma. If I could take back my words, I would. Periodically people saunter in for a beverage or a biscuit. I avoid their eyes and hope they don't make any conversation as I flip through the magazines on the coffee table. I pretend to be engrossed in the material even though my vision blurs the print. Each time the door is pushed open, my heart beats with hope as well as dread.

It seems like an eternity before Dr. Kilkenny walks in frowning and sits in the chair next to me. There's no one else in the room now.

"She okay?" I hold my breath.

"That's *not* how I hoped the meeting would go," Dr. Kilkenny says curtly.

"I wasn't thinking." My hands grip the faded armrests. "The lies are eating me up." I think that I have no more tears left, but I'm wrong.

Dr. Kilkenny sighs, grabs a tissue from a box on the table, and hands it to me. "It took a long time for your mother to trust me, and then the group, with the tough stuff. She may have told you someday. Or maybe not. We hadn't gotten there. Needless to say, it was a shock to her that you knew."

The truth remains bitter in my mouth. My shoulders slouch. "She'll probably never want to see me again." Tears continue to stream down my face.

Dr. Kilkenny softens her eyes and hands me another tissue. "Give her time."

Clutching my stomach, I say, "It was so hard waiting and not knowing if she'd ever see me. I don't know if I can do that again. My life's on hold. I don't know what to do."

"You'll have to figure out your own life, just as she's figuring out hers."

"It's not fair, you know," I say as I scrunch the tissues and toss them in the bin.

Dr. Kilkenny, with her greying hair pulled back in slides, peers over glasses resting on the bridge of her nose. "Tell me what's not fair."

"That I have to carry all this with me. I don't have a home anymore. My world is shattered, too. And she doesn't give a damn. Life was too hard. She wanted to be free. She tossed in the towel. I get all that. Now she wants to go off on her own, and to hell with how that affects anyone else." I glare at Dr. Kilkenny. Through gritted teeth, I say, "She's a selfish coward."

Dr. Kilkenny sits back in the chair and crosses her arms. Her blouse is buttoned high and her suit is impeccable. She says, "Sometimes you have to be selfish in order to take care of yourself."

I grab my bag and stand up. "I know I have to move on, but it's hard now that I know the truth." My ankle's stiff and it takes a second to get my footing. Reaching for my jacket on the back of the chair, I teeter a second, but catch myself.

Dr. Kilkenny rises. "I'll call you tomorrow to check in and tell you how your mother is doing." She looks tired as she touches my arm. "And to see how you're doing." I avoid her eyes as I mutter thanks and stuff my arms into the sleeves of my jacket. She stands back and lets me pass.

As I turn toward the door, I see Ma. She's standing in the entryway wearing an oversized sweater and hugging a book. Her face is ashen and her posture stooped.

Instantly Dr. Kilkenny is at Ma's side. "Where did you come from?"

"I was walking to the library and heard your voices." Ma looks down at the hardwood floor.

"Now's not the time." Dr. Kilkenny tries to steer her out of the room.

Ma doesn't move. "It is."

Dr. Kilkenny raises her voice. "I don't think you're ready for this. Not now."

Ma shakes her head and looks Dr. Kilkenny straight in the eyes. "I can do this." Her voice is soft, but firm.

"It's been a long day, Annie." Dr. Kilkenny puts her body between us.

Ma walks around Dr. Kilkenny and stands before me. Her eyes are bloodshot and puffy. "No. Now. Eliza's right. I've been a coward."

"I didn't mean that." I look down. "I'm just a git."

Dr. Kilkenny motions to a smaller room off the family lounge. "Let's at least go in here, where we can have some privacy." She walks over and flips on the overhead light. The room is barely large enough for the small round table and four chairs. There's no window, only wallpaper the color of moss.

Ma sits first, with her back to the closed door. The room smells like stale coffee. Dr. Kilkenny sits at Ma's side. I sit across from Ma. She pulls her sweater tighter, stares at the center of the table and says, "I made a choice, and I have to live with it." She swallows hard. "I'm sorry I hurt you. Never would I have wanted that. But it got too hard living with the lies. The pain. The loneliness. Death seemed easier." She looks up at me. "You're right. It was the coward's way out."

My voice cracks. "I didn't mean that."

Ma tilts her head back and closes her eyes. "All my life, I never felt I had any choices or power. Killing myself felt like power."

Dr. Kilkenny rests a hand over Ma's. Ma opens her eyes then, but stares at the ceiling. For a minute, she doesn't speak. Then she says, "I didn't see how my life would ever get better. Except maybe by dying."

I say, "I should have returned your call that morning. I was almost too late."

Ma turns her gaze from the ceiling to me. "I wanted to know how long you'd be gone, but you couldn't have stopped me. I would have done it at some point." The corners of her mouth turn upward slightly, but her eyes remain dull. "It was almost exciting planning it. I thought I picked the best time."

My gut sinks. "Your fortieth birthday, of all days?"

Ma shrugs. "Why not? It was just another day. And I didn't want to live the next forty years like the first forty."

I trace my finger along the surface of the table. It smells like lemon, sticky from layers of furniture polish. Beneath the glossy surface are cigarette burns, water marks and other stains. Placing my hands in my lap, I say in a lowered voice, "I had no idea about Grandma hurting you, let alone the horrible things Granda did."

Ma gasps. "What?"

Quickly I add, "Linda told me about Grandma."

"*Linda*?"

"Linda Gallagan. But now it's Linda Graham. Da said she was your friend in school. So I found her on the Internet. She lives here in Dublin and she teaches at the National Performing Arts Center. I met her, and she told me things."

"I haven't thought about her in years. We were close. A long time ago."

Dr. Kilkenny pushes back from the table. "It's been a long day. Why don't we find another time to talk?"

Ma shakes her head and looks straight at me. "You said you talked to a solicitor." Her voice quivers slightly. "I need to know what you've done."

Dr. Kilkenny fixes me with a cautionary look and sits back.

"It's a long story. Things came together when I found those pictures Granda took." Ma cringes. I say, "I found Clara McShane, a solicitor who sued the Church and made them pay for priests molesting boys. She suggested that I have the hairs tested."

"Hairs?" Dr. Kilkenny arches her brows.

I explain, "I found hairs in a plastic bag with my baby book, hidden in a suitcase of Ma's."

Ma covers her eyes. "I forgot about that."

Dr. Kilkenny looks back and forth between Ma and me. "Someone want to fill me in?"

"I was moving out of Da's and I needed one more suitcase so I found one of Ma's in our hall closet. That's where I found the bag of hairs and my baby book."

Dr. Kilkenny looks at Ma. "Your father's?"

Ma nods. "I thought maybe someone would believe me if I had evidence." She rolls her eyes and shakes her head. "I always watched those crime shows on the telly. But I didn't have the guts to tell anyone. I was scared. Who would believe me over him?"

"The solicitor did," I say. "Clara was brilliant. She had *him* by the short hairs. He won't bother you again. In fact, she made him pay."

"What? How?" says Ma.

"Granda signed over the titles to the guest cottages and the house in Naples to you. So you own those properties now. *Just you.* And Granda has to pay you rent to live in the Naples house—if you let him. Each month he'll send you the rent money to live on. Plus he wrote a check. It's big."

Ma's eyes widen.

I pull the check and the legal papers out of my bag and hand them to Ma. "Once I started putting the pieces together, I needed to make sure you'd never have to depend on anyone. You can use the money to start over. Here or anywhere."

Ma whispers, "He did this for me?"

I scowl. "He did it because we threatened to expose him.

Part of the agreement is that he can't have any contact with you. If he does, he'll pay more."

"I don't have to see him or talk to him again?" Ma asks.

"No," I say. "Only if you feel a need. *You're* in control."

Staring at the check and papers, Ma says, "I've never had anything of my own."

"Now you'll have plenty. Da can manage the cottages unless you want to sell them. Whatever. It's your choice. But, it's not something you have to decide right away. Granda's paying me and Da, too. He'll not bother *any* of us again."

There's a long pause.

Ma lowers her voice. "Does Seamus know about...?"

I shake my head. "When I was trying to sort things out—before I found the pictures that Granda took—Da agreed to DNA testing. But he never read the results. He burned them. I didn't tell him that I know he's not my father." I lean forward, resting my weight against the table, and it tilts. I lean back, cross my arms over my chest, and say, "I guess that's one secret I'm okay keeping. He's my da. He raised me."

Ma's shoulders relax, and she smiles. "He's a good man."

"I know that now." I pause. "Ma, I also know about Paddy. He agreed to the paternity test, too."

Beneath the dumpy, worn sweater, Ma's wearing the smart clothes Da bought her. She bites her lip, then says, "Seamus doesn't think I remember what happened with Paddy, but I do. I already suspected I might be pregnant when I got drunk that night." She laughs, but it's low and forced. "Paddy was a big talker, but he couldn't pull it off."

"But Da said he found you half naked in a pasture."

"I passed out from the drink after we tried. When Seamus

found me, he thought Paddy had, well, done it because he found Paddy's car keys there."

"You let Da think that?"

Ma nods. "It wasn't easy for me to seduce Seamus, but I managed one night, not too long after he found me. When I told him I was pregnant, he offered to marry me. It was my chance to get away from home and give you a proper father. We never talked about whether he or Paddy was the father."

"Did you know about Da and Paddy being...*close*...when you married Da?"

For a moment Ma stares at me open-mouthed, then turns her head toward the empty moss-colored wall. "I just thought that he was trying to protect his mate." Shifting in her chair, she bumps the table and it wobbles. "At one point, he said he would try to end the relationship. He loved you. I think he loved me, too. Just not in that way."

For the first time I notice that the bulging veins on Ma's hands look a little like Grandma's. I look down at the flat, mostly concealed veins on my hand. Her fingernails have a light polish on them while mine are unpolished.

I say, "I take it Da didn't know about your affair with Mr. Walters."

Ma looks like she's been slapped. She recoils and hugs herself. Instantly, my stomach knots. I look anxiously at Dr. Kilkenny, who says to Ma, "Annie, I insist we continue this visit another time. It's been too much." She stands and motions for me to do the same.

Ma covers her eyes with her the palms of her hands. "You know that too?"

I say, "Mr. Walters told me about the two of you. And

then I found your letters to him. He said he thought for years that he might be my father."

Ma doesn't move. Dr. Kilkenny purses her lips and sits back down.

Ma's voice is low. "When he could see that I was pregnant, he asked me if he was the father. Even though I didn't think so, I let him believe that he was."

"He said you loved him," I tell her.

Ma stares at the dingy wall. Her voice is flat as she says, "I thought I did. No one had ever shown me such affection. Willie gave me money to help you go to university. He knew your da and I couldn't afford to send you, and I was never going to ask my parents."

"The money in the baby book?" I said, remembering. "That was for me, for school?"

Ma nods.

I say, "He—Mr. Walters—took a DNA test, too."

Ma's shoulders droop. "Does *he* know?"

"Only that he's not my biological father."

Ma says, "I should give Willie the money back."

I lean forward. "Why the hell should you do that? Do you have any idea how many other girls Mr. Walters was involved with over the years?"

Ma shakes her head and looks away. "Linda tried to tell me there were others, but I didn't want to believe her."

A sour taste rises in my mouth. "It was wrong what he did. Keep the bloody money."

"You keep it. Do what you like with it," Ma says. "I don't want anything from him."

In the family lounge, a child wails. Voices cajole the child to settle down, and after a few minutes it's quiet again. A doctor is paged over the intercom. Dr. Kilkenny looks down at her folded hands.

Teary-eyed, Ma says, "It turns out that the people who were supposed to love me, hurt me. People I thought I could trust betrayed me. Only the people who didn't really love me never left me."

My family. Broken, but whole. Distant, but close.

Ma reaches for my hands across the table and straightens her spine. "I want to live the rest of my life the way *I* want to. I don't want to take care of anyone but *me* right now. That doesn't mean that I don't love you. I do, more than you know."

"You just don't need me anymore," I say and wipe my face with my sleeve.

With her gaze intense, Ma squeezes my hand. Her hands are warm and moist. She says, "You need to live your own life. Don't live it for me or anyone else. *You* have to choose now what you want to do. Not to please anyone. Not to take care of anyone." I push away from the table and go over and hug Ma. Our tears mingle when she presses her cheek against mine. As we hold each other, Ma says, "Live without regret. I know I'm going to from now on."

Chapter Thirty-Three

As the engines whine and the flight attendant talks through the usual emergency procedures, I take out my cell phone. There's a new text from Ryan. "I will miss you. Let me know when you land." I stare at it for a moment and then shut off the phone, stuff it into my bag, and rest my head against the window.

Next to me, in the middle seat, a woman bottle-feeds an infant. "For her ears, so they don't pop," she explains. The man on the aisle, wearing a business suit, buries his nose in a newspaper. I smile and take out my earphones to listen to the music that Ryan loaded onto my iPod for the trip, but hold the wires in my hand instead and look out the window just as the plane separates from the runway.

As the plane ascends, Dublin shrinks to a miniature city. Buildings and cars look like toys. The September sun slices through the clouds and ricochets off the surface of the Irish Sea.

"Are you going to visit family in New York?" asks my seatmate as she slips a pacifier into her baby's mouth.

"No," I say. "I've just always wanted to go to America. I'll travel, maybe visit some people I've met over the years. My family owns a bed-and-breakfast, and the American guests always invite us to come over."

"Lovely. Will you be gone long?" the woman asks.

"Hard to say." I reach down, yank my bag out from under the seat and I stuff the boarding pass of my one-way ticket inside it.

The plane barks steeply, making a u-turn to the west. Below, the sun shimmers off the water. As we pass over the coast, wispy clouds blanket the lush, green countryside and the rocky shoreline rimmed by white surf.

Then it is gone.

I settle into my seat, close my eyes, and try to envision a new future while committing to memory every detail of the home I'm leaving.

Acknowledgments

This book could not have been written or published without the love and support of my husband, David Graham. He has passionately encouraged my writing, spent countless hours reading and editing it, and cheered me to the finish line. It is his book as much as mine.

I am grateful to my family for their encouragement: my children, Andrew, Connor and Kate; my mother, Elizabeth Jane Pautz; and my sister, Liz Christopherson, who read the first draft with a keen eye and made invaluable suggestions.

Many friends have supported and assisted me on this journey: Jeanne Cotter; Janet DesLauriers Morris; Laura Braafladt; Judy Walker; Paula Baker; Char Mason; Joan O'Neill; Maggie Kirkpatrick; Sonia Cairns; Terrie Wheeler; Pat Hoven; Beth LaBreche; Terri Shepherd; Andrea Grazzini; Don McNeil; William Studer; and Anne Nicolai.

Finally, thank you to Mary Carroll Moore (writing instructor extraordinaire), the countless writers I've been privileged to know and learn from through classes at the Loft Literary Center and Madeline Island School of the Arts, and Ryan Scheife at Mayfly Design.